Elizabeth Gail
and the missing love letters

Hilda Stahl

WindRider BOOKS

Tyndale House Publishers, Inc., Wheaton, Illinois

Dedicated with love to Jeff and Kathy Stahl

The Elizabeth Gail Series

Fourth printing, December 1986

Library of Congress Catalog Card Number 81-85456
ISBN 0-8423-0709-5, paper
Copyright ©1982 by Hilda Stahl
All rights reserved
Printed in the United States of America

Contents

One
Exciting plans

Elizabeth leaned against her school locker and her eyes sparkled as she once again read her letter from Scott Norris. He was coming for Thanksgiving! In two weeks she'd see him again! Her heart leaped with excitement; then she quickly stuffed the letter inside her English book before anyone grabbed it from her and read it. It would be just like Jerry Grosbeck to do that. He'd been acting very strangely toward her lately. She frowned. Several years ago when they'd lived in the same foster home she'd called him Gross Jerry Grosbeck. If he didn't quit teasing her and acting so funny, she'd start calling him that again. Didn't he know that she was fourteen years old, and not a little girl now?

With her pointed chin high Elizabeth walked down the noisy hallway. It was time for her independent study hour when she practiced piano. She forced away the dreamy smile in case anyone was looking at her and guessed that she was in love. Jill knew and the twins had guessed. Once Susan had said something, then had forgotten to say any more. She'd been too involved with Joe Wilkens.

"Libby! Hey, Libby! Wait for me!"

She turned with a frown. How many times did she have to remind Jill to call her Elizabeth? How could a concert pianist be called Libby? She was legally Elizabeth Gail Johnson and not Libby Dobbs, aid kid, anymore.

Jill flipped her long hair over her slender shoulder and moistened her pink lips with the tip of her tongue. "Don't frown, Libby. I have great news!"

Elizabeth fell into step beside Jill and wondered if the other students watched them as they walked side by side. They were probably the tallest girls in school. "What news, Jill?"

Jill took a deep breath and her dark eyes sparkled. "Ben asked me to go to the concert with him Saturday night!"

Elizabeth gasped, stopping dead. "Ben? My brother Ben?"

Jill laughed and nodded her head. "I could barely believe it myself. He asked me just a while ago and I didn't squeal or anything. I just said that I'd love to go and that I'd be ready by six." She rolled her eyes and hugged her books tightly. "Libby, I have waited six months for this day! I'm so glad I lost that last ten pounds! Mom said I could go shopping after school Friday. Now, I'll have something special to shop for."

Elizabeth laughed softly as they walked toward the piano room. "I have news, too, Jill." Elizabeth stopped at the closed door and her hazel eyes twinkled. She could almost feel Scott's letter burning through the cover of her English book. "Scott is coming for Thanksgiving! I can't wait! I haven't seen him since summer vacation, and then for only a day. And Mom said that her brother and his wife and cousin Rhonda will be coming also. That leaves Scott free to spend more time with me."

"Maybe he'll tell you he loves you," whispered Jill breathlessly. "I bet he does love you. I bet he doesn't care that he's already twenty and you're only fourteen."

Elizabeth's stomach tightened and a thrill ran down her spine. If only Scott loved her! Maybe once she told him about the piano competition that she was in, he'd admire her so much that his feelings would turn into love. Music was as important to him as it was to her.

The bell buzzed and Elizabeth jumped.

She hurried inside as Jill said she'd see her later on the bus.

Cold rain lashed against the window as Elizabeth opened her piano book and set it in place. She'd practice her concert piece and her finger exercises, and she'd be the best pianist in the competition. Surely Scott would love her if she won.

She smiled as she touched the keys of the baby grand. She played "Theme from the Surprise Symphony" by Haydn, thrilling deep inside that she was actually playing the piano in such a way. Chuck and Vera had said from the time she'd come to live with them that she had a special talent for piano. Her lips curved into a smile at the thought of her two great dreams. One was to be adopted by the Johnson family and the other to be a famous concert pianist. Shortly after her thirteenth birthday she'd been adopted and Susan was now her sister and Ben, Kevin, and Toby were her brothers. The Johnson farm was as much a part of her as it was of them. They had prayed her into their family, and she was glad!

She turned, then stopped short. "Jerry Grosbeck! When did you come in?" She frowned at him impatiently, but he smiled at her and walked around to lean his long, thin body against the piano. He was

8

dressed in dark gray cords and a light blue pullover sweater.

"I heard you playing and I had to come in and hear you." He smiled and she automatically smiled back. "You play better than any words I can think of, Libby."

"Elizabeth."

"I guess it's been Libby for so long that I don't know if I can change." He touched a low C, then looked at Libby and smiled again, smiled as if he were very proud of her. She couldn't understand him and she wanted to tell him to leave her alone so she could practice. She stared at her Hanon exercise book and tried to think of a polite way to tell him to get lost.

He stood up and looped his thumbs in his back pockets. "Please play for me."

She flushed and her fingers felt very stiff. "I'm only practicing."

"I am your greatest fan, Libby. Can't you play something just for me? I'll leave as soon as you do."

She shook her head. "I'll play for you another time, Jerry. I really need to practice now." Why couldn't he leave?

"You're going to make it, Libby." He gently tapped her shoulder and she jerked back. "You are going to be a famous concert pianist. You'll forget all about the beatings you got from your real mother.

You'll forget all about the terrible foster homes you lived in, and you'll even take for granted that you're wanted and loved."

Tears filled her eyes as she stared into Jerry's solemn face. "Jerry, I want to forget all that. There are whole days that go by now when I do forget, but someday I want to put it right out of my memory forever! And I'll never take love for granted. I'm thankful that I'm loved! I'm thankful that I'm a Christian and that I know about God's love. I will make it as a concert pianist! I will make it because of my new family and their love and God's love! I *will* make it!"

Suddenly Jerry leaned down and kissed her trembling lips, then turned and hurried out. She stared at the closed door, her hazel eyes wide in amazement. What had made him kiss her? She touched her lips gingerly, then frowned. She would forget about that kiss. She wanted only Scott's kisses, not Gross Jerry Grosbeck's.

"He'd better never try that again or he'll have a black eye from me," she muttered as she opened the book of finger exercises. She wouldn't think about Jerry another minute! This hour was for practice, not conversation or stray thoughts.

Her fingers flew up and down the keys, and she remembered how she'd played her first fumbling song on the Johnson's piano when she was eleven years old. After hours and hours of practice she could play smoothly and with feeling. Before Thanksgiving she'd practice even more so that Scott would stand beside her and admire her playing and praise her, maybe even kiss her. She flushed and her hands dropped to her lap. She absently rubbed her hands along her dark green dress pants, then tugged at the collar of her knit shirt.

Would Scott notice how mature she looked now? She didn't have a great body like Susan, but she wasn't a skinny stringbean any longer. And with her new curly perm, her hair always looked good.

Suddenly the door burst open and Elizabeth jerked around in alarm. At the sight of Susan standing there with tears streaming down her face, Elizabeth jumped to her feet and hurried to Susan.

"What's wrong? Are you hurt?"

Susan pressed her hands to her wet cheeks and her chest rose and fell in agitation. "Joe and I just broke up," she whispered brokenly. "What will I do without Joe?"

"Oh, Susan." Elizabeth wrapped her long arms around Susan and held her close. The top of Susan's red-gold head just reached Elizabeth's chin. Her peach-colored sweater felt soft. "Don't cry. Now you can go with

11

all the boys who've been after you."

Susan sniffed loudly and pulled away. "I won't go with anyone! I hate boys! All they do is break your heart!" She tugged her sweater over her cords, then brushed the tears off her cheeks. "How can I face anyone? How can I go to Spanish class and sit next to Joe without breaking down?"

"You can do it. You know God is always with you to help you."

Susan pushed her long hair back with both hands, then nodded. "You're right, Elizabeth. I know you're right and as soon as I calm down I'll be able to go to Spanish class." She shuddered, then wrapped her arms around herself as if she were freezing. "Never fall in love, Elizabeth."

Elizabeth looked down quickly at the English book on the piano bench and thought of the letter from Scott Norris. Susan's advice was too late. "I'll remember that, Susan."

"How can I live without Joe Wilkens?" Fresh tears streamed down her face and she quickly turned away, her shoulders drooping and her head bent.

Elizabeth picked up her English book and touched the letter from Scott. Someday he'd love her as much as she loved him. He'd never break her heart the way Joe had broken Susan's!

Two
Joanne's news

Elizabeth turned to face Rachael Avery, trying to see by the expression on her face how well she'd played the song. A weak sun added just a touch of brightness to the plants hanging in the window of Rachael's music room.

Rachael sighed deeply as she clasped her hands in her lap. "Elizabeth, in a few years you'll win the Van Cliburn Award!"

Elizabeth's eyes widened and her heart leaped. "Do you really think so, Rachael? Honestly?"

Rachael nodded as she smoothed her skirt over her knees. "I almost won a few years ago. The competition was stiff! My, but I enjoyed being there to play for the judges!" She clasped Elizabeth's long, slender hand. "In a few years you'll be better than I was at my best. You'll be known worldwide. Never, never allow anything to dim your dream!"

Elizabeth felt as if she could float. Just wait until she told Scott. He would be so proud of her! "Rachael, nothing will keep me from my piano!"

"I know. I knew it from the moment I first met you when you were twelve. I could see it in your eyes and hear it in your voice. You may even give an Elizabeth Johnson Award someday."

Elizabeth laughed and wondered how many of her foster parents would recognize her now as the ragged, skinny aid kid with the foul mouth and nasty disposition. Suddenly she wanted to tell all the hopeless kids of the world that they could become anything they wanted to if they worked at it. Someday she'd give an award to underprivileged kids who fought to fulfill a dream! She would tell them that it could be done no matter what the circumstances.

She flushed as she realized Rachael was trying to get her attention. "Sorry," she mumbled with her head down and her face hot.

"The competition is going to be at the Cramer Auditorium on December 30 at ten o'clock. There are twenty-five piano students who qualify to enter. The youngest is twelve and the oldest, sixteen." Rachael leaned forward earnestly. "You have a good chance to win, Elizabeth, but it'll take a lot of practice between now and then. Let's go over the piece again. I want you to become involved with the music so that you're a part of it, so that you feel it. I want you to play for the joy of playing, even with the judges and the audience listening to you."

Elizabeth nodded, unable to speak around the lump in her throat. Tears blurred her vision as she looked at the pictures on the wall of Rachael in concert. Did Rachael ever regret giving up concerts to be a wife and mother?

"Play the piece again, Elizabeth, and watch this right here." She tapped the music with her yellow pencil as Elizabeth poised her fingers on the keys.

The music echoed inside Elizabeth for the rest of Saturday, and she could still hear it in her mind as she sat beside Jill in Sunday school class. It was hard to concentrate on the lesson Bill Voss was teaching. Once she heard Bill ask a question and Jerry Grosbeck answered. Elizabeth's back stiffened and she forced back a blush as she remembered that terrible moment when he'd kissed her.

How could she talk to him after what he'd done? Why had he kissed her? He was acting crazier than ever.

Suddenly Jill nudged Elizabeth and she jumped in surprise.

"Class is over and it's time to go into church. What are you dreaming about this time?" Jill lifted her dark brows. "As if I need to ask."

"Let's get out of here quick!" whispered Elizabeth urgently.

"Why? Aren't we sitting with the others the way we always do?" Jill hurried along beside Elizabeth down the hallway toward the sanctuary.

"Not today! I mean it, Jill." Elizabeth paused and looked over her shoulder. Jerry was looking at her! She took a deep breath, rushed around Brenda Wilkens, and hurried to the back of the church. Today she and Jill would not sit three rows from the front with the other teens. She wouldn't stay in the same church building with Jerry if she could help it.

After the service Elizabeth hurried to the station wagon, knowing that Jill wanted to find out what was going on. Not even Jill would learn about Jerry's kiss!

"Why won't you talk to me, Libby?"

She spun around with a glare. "Will you please call me Elizabeth, Jill? If you forget again, I won't even answer you."

"What is wrong with you? What did I do? Why won't you tell me what's really bothering you? You never keep secrets from me and I never keep any from you." Jill

16

folded her arms across her chest and frowned.

"Yes, Libby, what is wrong?"

She gasped and spun around to find Jerry standing with Ben. She wanted to vanish into thin air. "I want to go home and eat. Do you mind?"

Jerry laughed and she saw his eyes twinkle mischievously. Did Ben or Jill notice?

"Are you nervous about the competition?" asked Ben anxiously. "You don't need to be, Elizabeth. I've heard you play your piece, and I know you know you'll win! As long as you keep practicing and don't let anything interfere. And I'll see that you don't!"

She knew he meant it and she smiled thankfully. Maybe she should tell him about Jerry's strange actions so that he could have a talk with Jerry. She bit the inside of her bottom lip. She couldn't say anything about Jerry to Ben. They were good friends. "I just want to get home and eat dinner. Mom has a ham in the oven."

Ben said he couldn't wait to eat either and Jill said that she'd better get to the car before her family left her behind. Jerry only looked at Elizabeth and laughed as if to say he knew what she'd done.

"I hear you have company coming for

Thanksgiving," said Jerry, looking right at Elizabeth.

She clutched her Bible tighter. Did Jerry mean Scott? Had he somehow read Scott's letter?

"We're having a houseful," said Ben as he zipped his jacket almost to his chin. A breeze ruffled his red hair.

Elizabeth listened and watched Jerry's face covertly for his reactions. She saw a muscle tighten in his jaw when Ben mentioned Scott Norris. Didn't Jerry like Scott?

Finally Jerry told Ben good-bye, then said to her, "See you in school tomorrow."

"All right." Not if she could help it! She slipped into the back seat of the station wagon and pushed her hands into her coat sleeves. She wouldn't think another minute about Jerry Grosbeck! She'd think about the next love letter that she would write to Scott. If she didn't find time today, she'd write it after school Monday.

She thought off and on about the letter Sunday and Monday in school. Maybe she'd have a little time during the lunch break if Jill left her alone long enough.

Fifteen minutes before the bell rang, Ben asked Jill to walk with him so they could talk, and Elizabeth thankfully pulled out her pad of paper.

"I have some news that you'll just love, Libby Dobbs."

She looked up with a frown, almost snapping the pencil in half as she watched Joanne sit down across from her. "I am not Libby Dobbs and you know it. I am Elizabeth Johnson."

Joanne wrinkled her pretty nose and shook back her long blonde hair. "I have news."

"So you said." Elizabeth closed her pad and locked her hands together on top of it. With Joanne around, Scott's letter would have to wait.

Joanne squared her shoulders and looked very pleased with herself. "I am in the piano competition at Cramer Auditorium."

Elizabeth's heart sank.

"Only twenty-five people are competing, twenty-five of the best students in the area. Maybe next year you'll be good enough."

Elizabeth lifted her pointed chin. "I'm in it this year."

"What?" Joanne's mouth dropped open and her eyes widened in surprise. "You? There must be a mistake!"

Elizabeth's stomach tightened and she leaned forward. "I am in it, Joanne, and I mean to win!"

Joanne tipped back her head and laughed. Elizabeth felt as if a hundred pairs of eyes were staring at them and she quickly pushed back her chair and stood up.

Joanne jumped up and the smile was gone. Her blue eyes were icy as she glared at Elizabeth. "I'll see about that! My mother is going to be very angry about this. You wait and see! She'll get you out. She knows that I'll win, but she would never agree for us to compete. You are not in my league!"

She said a whole lot more as Elizabeth rushed down the hall trying to get away. Finally she turned to Joanne, her eyes narrowed. "Joanne, leave me alone! I am not going to fight with you. I just know that I'm in the competition and I know that I can win. If you won't compete with me, then drop out!"

Joanne gasped, then turned with a swish of her skirt and hurried away.

Elizabeth sagged against a locker and closed her eyes. A hand touched her arm and she jerked up to find Jerry standing beside her, his face full of concern.

"Did Joanne hurt you again, Libby? I'd like to tell that girl a few things and I will one of these days if she doesn't leave you alone!"

Elizabeth smiled weakly. "Thanks, Jerry, but I'm all right. She just learned that we're in the same piano competition and she's not happy."

"Too bad for her! When will she learn that you're the best?"

Elizabeth laughed and a strange warmth spread through her. "Thanks, Jerry." She couldn't think of anything else to say but just smiled up at him, then hurried away as the bell rang.

Three
Letter to Scott

Dear Scott,

I love you! You are my life and I couldn't live without you. A few minutes ago I pretended that you were sitting in the family room with me, and I played my concert piece for you, "Theme from the Surprise Symphony" by Haydn. I pretended that you enjoyed it so much that you swept me off the piano bench into your arms and kissed me.

I wish you were here right now.

Susan and Joe broke up. She says that he likes April Brakie. April and May are the identical twins that you met when you were here. I know April likes Joe, but I don't think she'll go with him because of Susan. Susan spends most of her time crying. I would cry, too, if you didn't love me and broke up with me.

Ben asked Jill to go to the concert with him last Saturday night. Jill can't talk about anything but Ben now. She's forgotten that she's writing a book. Maybe she doesn't want to be a famous writer anymore. And Ben said the group sang two of your songs. He said he wanted to tell everyone around that he knew Scott Norris, the famous songwriter. If I'd been there, I'd have stood up and said that I knew you and that you write the best gospel music around.

I wanted to go to the concert really bad, but I had to stay home to practice. With the competition only a few weeks away I have to practice every minute. But I will have time to be with you on Thanksgiving Day. We will take a long walk and just talk. I want to hear about your new songs. I want to know if your parents and sisters feel better about you quitting college. Dad said he could understand how important it was to them that you become a doctor, but he said it is more important for you to be what God has planned for your life. I'm sure your family knows that.

Yesterday after Sunday dinner, I rode Snowball and Ben rode Star and we checked on Ben's Christmas trees. This year Kevin and Toby are joining the Christmas tree business with Ben.

It was cold riding, but so far it hasn't

snowed. We saw several deer and I wanted you to be with me so you could see how they ran into the trees so gracefully.

I still can't believe that Ben took out my very best friend. He used to ignore her, but now he really likes her. And she's almost as tall as he is. She says his red hair is beautiful. I guess it is, but I like your brown hair better.

You do love me, don't you, Scott? I want you to think I'm beautiful even though I'm not. Susan is. All the boys think so, but nobody thinks I am but you and Dad.

Remember I told you about Joanne Tripper? She thinks she's so great! She really believes that she's going to win the competition December 30. I hope she gets last place!

I know I'm not supposed to feel that way since I'm a Christian, but I do! Joanne is good on the piano, but she acts so big! She can't talk without bragging. She says her mother knows two of the judges and that she's sure to win. Then she said even without those two judges she'd win. She said she's going to wear a new dress that will make everyone look at her. She will, too! She always dresses so the boys stare at her. She says she could be Miss America if she tried. I wish she would do that and forget about piano!

On Thanksgiving Day I'm going to kiss

you in front of everyone. I want them all to know that we love each other. Someday we'll get married and I will travel all over the world doing concerts and you'll write more songs and maybe even come with me on tour. We'll be very happy.

Kevin just turned thirteen. He's lost most of his baby fat and he's very happy with himself. Mom bought him contact lenses and he looks so different! He's been studying how to be a detective and I feel him watching me all the time. Once he almost caught me writing a love letter to you. He and Toby would really tease me if they read one of the letters. These love letters are for only you, Scott. I never want anyone else to read them.

Toby finally has a best friend. A new family moved in where Brian and Lisa Parr lived. Jacob Braden and Toby became friends right off, and Toby sure thinks he's big. He was a little jealous of Kevin because he's had a best friend ever since Paul Noteboom has lived down the road from us. Paul is always ready to do anything Kevin suggests, and that had better not be spying on me!

Oh, Scott, I can't wait to see you! We'll have such a good time together! I love you. I love you. I love you.

With all my love and kisses,
Elizabeth Gail Johnson

Elizabeth held the letter to her heart and closed her eyes. If only she could send this to Scott! Last winter she'd told him she loved him and he'd been surprised, but then he'd kissed her and he knew she'd love him forever even if he didn't love her back.

She remembered how he'd smiled at her this summer and her heart leaped. Maybe he did love her a little. She swallowed hard as she thought about the courage it had taken for her to ask if he'd write to her if she wrote to him. He'd agreed and often she wondered if it had been just out of politeness.

Slowly she opened the middle drawer of her desk and reached to the back and pulled out a yellow folder with a flower drawn with red ink on it. Her stomach tightened and she glanced toward her closed-and-locked bedroom door. No one must see this folder or read the love letters inside!

Carefully she laid the letter she'd just written on the pile of love letters, then closed the folder, and slipped it back in the drawer. She rubbed her hand down her jeans, then reached for a clean sheet of paper.

Dear Scott,

I am glad that you can come to our house for Thanksgiving. You can sing your new songs for us. Maybe our family will ride out in the wagon while you are here. Uncle Steve and Aunt Ellen are also coming for Thanksgiving along with cousin Rhonda. We'll have a lot of fun. I'll play the piano for you if you want.

I'm entering a piano competition on December 30. Rachael Avery, my piano teacher, says that I have a good chance. I hope I win, but I might not since there are twenty-four others playing who might be better than I.

Ben and Jill went to a concert Saturday night and they said the group sang two of your songs. Ben said they were the best songs of the night. I couldn't go because I had to practice piano.

Thank you for taking time to write to me. I like to read your letters. I'll see you on Thanksgiving Day.

Your friend,
Elizabeth Gail Johnson

With a sigh Elizabeth folded the letter and addressed the envelope, then slipped the letter inside and stamped it. She pressed her lips to it and wished she could tell Scott that she'd sent him a kiss.

She walked from her room with the letter in her hand, wishing with all her heart that the other letter were inside the envelope instead of inside the folder in her desk drawer.

Someday Scott would love her. He just had to!

Four
Trouble

Elizabeth slipped her arms around Snowball's neck and Snowball neighed a happy welcome. She looked fat in her white winter hair. "Maybe I'll have time to ride you later, Snowball. I have to eat lunch now."

Snowball pressed close to the wooden fence and bobbed her head up and down. The cold wind whistled around the barn as Elizabeth rubbed Snowball's flank.

"I did fantastic this morning at my piano lesson. Rachael said I'm better than last week, and she thought I was good then. I can't wait for Scott to come hear me play! Oh, Snowball! Scott will be here in five days! I'll be able to look at him and hear him talk, and maybe even touch him!"

29

Quickly she looked around to make sure her family hadn't heard her. No one was outdoors and nothing moved except Goosy Poosy. The big white goose was part of the Johnson family, but he couldn't understand what she said. And even if he could, he couldn't repeat it, not even to Kevin or Toby.

Just then Elizabeth looked up and caught a movement at her bedroom window. She froze in her tracks, her eyes wide in alarm. Who was in her room? And why?

Scott's love letters! What if someone found those letters and read them? What if someone sent them to Scott?

Her face burned and her stomach tightened painfully as she raced to the back door of the large white house. Her hand slipped off the storm door handle and she frantically reached for it again.

Maybe no one was in her room. Maybe she had only imagined it. No one was supposed to go into another person's room without permission.

She jerked off her boots and coat and dropped them in a heap as she rushed through the back porch where coats and boots were kept. Her mouth felt too dry to swallow and her heart bumped painfully. If someone was in her room, he'd be in big trouble!

As she hurried past the grandfather clock, the deep tick-tick sounded like her own heartbeats. Lunch smells drifted from the kitchen as she sped up the carpeted stairs and down the hallway to her bedroom.

Panting, her chest rising and falling, she stopped in her open doorway. Toby and his friend Jacob stood near her desk. Toby held the puzzle box that her real dad had given her for her twelfth birthday. She leaped across the room and grabbed it from him.

He blinked in surprise, then turned red with embarrassment. "I just wanted to show Jacob the puzzle box."

"Get out!" She could barely speak around her rage. "Get out! Now!" Had they found the letters? Had they read them and laughed?

"Don't be mad, Elizabeth," said Jacob, his face pale. "I asked Toby to show it to me. I never saw one before. And I. . . ." His voice trailed away and he looked helplessly at Toby.

Toby grabbed his arm and tugged him from the room, slamming the door behind them. Elizabeth stared at the door a long time, then looked down at the box. Her knuckles were white from gripping it so tightly and she slowly relaxed her fingers.

Her legs gave way and she dropped into her chair at the desk. She closed her eyes and gulped great gulps of air. What if they had seen her letters? How could she survive if they had?

Finally she pulled open the desk drawer, her body trembling. Oh, she couldn't look!

Suddenly the door burst open, and Elizabeth slammed the drawer shut.

"Libby! Libby! What can I do?" Susan pressed against the wall, her face pale, her fists doubled at her sides.

Elizabeth wanted to yell at Susan to get out, but she couldn't. Susan looked very upset. "What's wrong?" Elizabeth walked slowly toward Susan.

"Joe's here! I walked down to the basement to get something for Mom, and Joe was down there with Ben. And they were playing Ping-Pong." Her voice ended in a wail. "Ping-Pong!"

Elizabeth knew how many hours Joe and Susan had spent playing Ping-Pong together the past two years, and even before that when they'd only been casual friends.

"He acts as if nothing is different! He just smiled and said hi to me and served the ball!" Susan pressed her hands to her cheeks. Her blue eyes were wide and filled with pain. Elizabeth stood helplessly in front of her.

"Shall I tell him to go home?" asked Elizabeth.

Susan gasped. "No! Don't you dare! I don't want him to think I can't be around him!"

Elizabeth shrugged. "Then go watch him play. Maybe Ben will beat him and you can laugh."

Susan burst into tears and covered her face with trembling hands. "You don't understand," she mumbled. "Nothing like this has ever happened to you."

Elizabeth thought of the love letters and what she'd do if the family or Scott read them, and she knew she had more reason to be upset than Susan ever could.

"What am I going to do?" wailed Susan as she dropped down on the big, round red hassock.

Elizabeth glanced nervously toward her desk, then back at Susan. "Just find a new boyfriend."

"Oh, sure. I could find one right out in the backyard."

"Call Adam. He'd come over and pretend to be your boyfriend."

Susan frowned. "Joe knows Adam likes May Brakie. Oh, sometimes I wish those Brakie twins had stayed away from here!"

Elizabeth looked down at the dark pink carpet and fought against the flush that threatened to turn her neck and face red. She knew Susan was really blaming her. If she hadn't lived at the Johnson farm, the twins would've stayed away. They came for help and a home. At least Chuck had been able to find them a Christian home even though there wasn't room for them to live with the Johnsons. Finally Elizabeth looked at Susan. "I hope you aren't going to say anything to the twins and hurt them."

Susan sniffed hard and rubbed tears away. "I won't, Libby. I like the girls. They can't help it if the boys like them."

"Boys like you, too," said Elizabeth sharply.

Susan sighed and stood up. "I know. I guess it just doesn't matter anymore. I guess I'll have Mom give me piano lessons so I can forget everything but piano like you do."

Elizabeth frowned. "You have to have a better reason than that to play the piano, Susan."

"Oh."

"I play because I can't *not* play! It's something inside me." She struggled for words, then flushed hotly. "I can't explain what I feel or mean, Susan."

"I don't understand, Libby. Nothing can be that important. I wouldn't want it to be. I'd have to give up too much to follow that kind of dream."

"But I'm not giving up anything! I don't care most of the time that I have to practice while you do other kinds of things or while you go with boys. My day is not right if I don't play the piano!" How could Susan not understand?

Susan slowly opened the bedroom door as she pushed her red-gold hair away from her pale face. "I think I'll go to my room and be alone awhile." She shuddered, then turned and walked out, leaving the door wide open.

Abruptly Elizabeth closed, then locked the door. Before she could rush to the desk to check on her precious love letters, she heard Mom call her. She hesitated, then unlocked the door and hurried downstairs.

Vera stood at the bottom of the stairs with a frown on her face. She leaned her elbows on the newel post. "Elizabeth, I can't find the dictionary. I'm working on the church newsletter and I need to look up a word. Do you know where it is?"

Elizabeth wanted to scream in anger and rush back to her room to the letters, but she managed to shake her head calmly. "I think Toby had it last. He was going to do his history report." Toby! He would be very sorry if her letters were gone or out of order!

Just then Kevin walked out of the family room. "I think this is the time for

Detective Johnson to get to work, Mom. I'll find the dictionary for you, and I'll find it in time for you to finish the newsletter today."

Vera laughed and Elizabeth managed a smile.

Kevin tapped his front tooth with his finger and wrinkled his brow in thought. "Where should I look first? Who should I ask? Ah! Toby! I'll start with him!" He hurried away and Vera laughed again and raised her eyebrows.

"I wonder if we can make it through this," she said as she tugged her knit shirt over her jeans. "Kevin seems to turn up whenever anything is out of the way."

Elizabeth stiffened. Would Kevin dare go in her room and do detective work and find her love letters? She turned to leave, but Vera stopped her.

"Please call the kids in for lunch."

Lunch! Who could eat at a time like this? "I'll eat later, Mom."

"Lunch is ready now, Libby. Call the others."

With a sigh Elizabeth walked toward the basement where she knew Ben was. Later she'd look at her letters. And if anything were out of place, someone would be very, very sorry!

Five
A visit from Jerry

Finally Elizabeth hung up the dish towel,
then checked to see what cycle the
dishwasher was on. As soon as it was on
dry, she'd shut it off and open the door to
let out the hot air.

She turned on the faucet until the water
was cold, then grabbed a glass of water and
drank thirstily. Now, she'd go upstairs and
look at her love letters to Scott. Nothing
would stop her this time! She'd ask Susan
to take care of the dishwasher.

Suddenly Ben walked into the kitchen
with a handful of mail. Jerry Grosbeck
walked in after him and Elizabeth felt her
shoulders tense.

"Hi, Libby." Jerry smiled and she wanted
to brush past him and run to her room, but
she forced herself to greet him.

"You have a letter, Elizabeth," said Ben,
holding out a white envelope.

Eagerly she took the envelope, wondering

who had written. Maybe her real grandma or maybe Grandma and Grandpa Johnson. She looked at the return address, then cried in happy surprise, "It's from Scott Norris! I didn't think he would write back so fast!" She pressed the letter to her heart, then suddenly realized the boys were looking at her, watching her. She caught a strange look on Ben's face, then saw a pained look on Jerry's. Had Ben guessed that she loved Scott? Oh, how dreadful! And why should Jerry look hurt? He shouldn't care if she got a letter from Scott Norris.

With her head high she walked past them, the letter clutched in her hand at her side.

The letter was jerked from her hand and she spun around with a scream. "Give that back right now, Jerry! That's my letter!" She lunged for it, but he jumped back and held it out of her reach. She was tall, but he was taller and his reach higher.

"Is this a love letter, Libby? I think I'll read it."

She turned to Ben in anguish. "Make him give it back, Ben. Please." She knew she would burst into tears any minute, and she just couldn't let that happen.

"We'll give it back after we read it," said Ben with a scowl. "We want to see what's in the letter to make you so happy."

"No!" She knew nothing was in the letter

that they couldn't read, but she wanted it to be a private letter that she could cherish and dream over. "I want that letter now!"

Jerry leaned toward her with a wicked grin. "Give me a kiss and I'll give you the letter."

"A kiss!" She swung her hand to slap his face hard, but once again he jumped back and the swing almost jerked her off balance. She staggered, then leaped at Jerry, grabbing the front of his shirt. His arm snaked around her small waist and tightened so that she was pressed against him. Her heart jumped and a shiver ran down her back. She stopped struggling and looked at Jerry as if she'd never seen him before.

"A kiss first," he said barely above a whisper.

In a daze she touched her lips to his cheek, then took the letter he offered with lifeless fingers and fled to her bedroom. She leaned against the closed door, her hazel eyes wide, her heart racing at top speed. What was wrong with her? Why had she kissed Jerry instead of kicking him in the shin? She looked at the letter and her mouth went dry. Now Ben and Jerry knew how important a letter from Scott was to her. What if Ben told Scott how she'd acted? Scott had no idea that she still loved him. She knew he thought she'd just said

39

she loved him last winter on the spur of the moment and that she'd soon gotten over the idea.

She pressed her hand to her burning cheek and groaned. He'd stop writing to her if he knew she still loved him.

She breathed deeply, then sat at her desk and slowly, awkwardly opened the letter. What if he'd changed his mind about Thanksgiving? Oh, that must not happen!

She read through the letter, then laughed in delight. Scott was coming for the Thanksgiving weekend instead of just the day! Four days with Scott Norris! She closed her eyes and kissed the letter happily. This was just too good to be true!

She held the letter high and twirled around the room, her long legs almost grazing the furniture. Finally she sat down at her desk and pulled out her writing pad. She gripped her yellow ball-point pen and wrote:

Dear Scott,

I love you! I know you are coming for the Thanksgiving weekend because you love me. We will have such a good time together! Each day we'll go for a ride or hike, and we'll talk and talk. I have a lot to tell you about the piano competition. Rachael says that if I keep improving I'll win or come close. With your encouraging me to practice, I know I'll win.

And if you attend the competition, I'll play just for you and then I'll win for sure.

I'm glad you're not like Jerry Grosbeck. I don't think you met him. He's a friend of Ben's, but I don't like him much at all. We used to be in a foster home together when I was little. He has a scar on the side of his face that he got from his dad slashing him with a broken beer bottle. Now he lives with a Christian family and he is a Christian, too. Most of the time I can't stand him, but sometimes he is nice. Once he stopped Joanne Tripper from picking on me. He's on the basketball team at school. I watched him play only once. I guess girls like him, but he doesn't pay any attention to them. He should be a sophomore or a junior, but he flunked too much so he's a freshman with me. He's in three of my classes. I think he's smarter than I am. He's sure been acting funny lately. He's always watching me. And he talks to me every chance he gets. I don't know why. It makes me feel sort of strange. I don't like him!

Susan is still feeling terrible about Joe. She needs to find a new boyfriend. Maybe Jerry. I guess that wouldn't be a good idea. Just writing about it makes me feel funny. I wonder if he thinks she's pretty? I bet he does; everyone else does. I wonder if she would like to go with him? I sure never thought about it before. Susan is probably too much in love with Joe yet to even look at Jerry. I guess she'd better not think about Jerry. I don't think she's too good for him or anything. I just don't think they'd suit each other. He's so tall and she's so short. I guess he needs a tall girl friend, and one who doesn't care that he was an aid kid. He used to be always dirty and ragged just like me. When we lived in the same foster home, we fought over the food because there was never enough to eat. I'm glad we both have happy homes now. I just wish I knew why he's acting so funny. I guess I've talked enough about Jerry Grosbeck.

I can't wait to see you again, Scott. It seems like a year instead of three months ago. Five more days and I'll see you again! Do you still look the same? I love your dark brown hair and blue eyes. Jerry's hair is almost as dark as yours, but he has brown eyes and he's almost as tall as you. He's not done growing yet. I think I'm done growing. I hope so! I'm taller than all but two boys in my class. Jill and I are the tallest girls in school except for Bebe Larsen and she's six feet. I get teased about being so tall and thin by some of the kids, but I don't mind too much. I can still be a famous concert pianist.

I just can't wait to see you! I love you. I love you. I love you!

> With all my love and kisses,
> Elizabeth Gail Johnson

She looked at the words "love" and "kisses" and frowned. She had given Jerry Grosbeck a kiss! A band tightened around her head. Why had she kissed Jerry? She had done a lot of dumb things, but that was the dumbest!

Suddenly she picked up the letter she'd just written and ripped it into tiny pieces and dropped it into her red wastebasket.

Why even write a letter to Scott now since she'd see him in five days? He probably couldn't care less that she wrote to him. Maybe he even read her letters and chuckled over them because she was a little girl and he was a grown man.

She rammed Scott's letter to her into the top desk drawer, then rushed from the bedroom. She'd play the piano and forget her mixed-up thoughts and feelings.

By the time she'd played for a half hour she felt more like herself. She managed a smile as she turned the page in her book to the "Blue Danube Waltz" by Johann Strauss Jr. When she finished playing she turned on the bench to give a bow to an imaginary audience and stopped in surprise. Jerry Grosbeck sat in Chuck's chair, listening to her!

"Shall I clap?" he asked softly with a smile.

"I didn't know you were here." She bit her lip and wondered what she should do.

"I sneaked in just after you started playing."

"Where's Ben?" Why hadn't he stayed

43

with Ben, away from her?

"He's putting a model together in the basement." He crossed his long legs. "I'm ready to hear more music."

She knew she couldn't play with him listening. "You go right ahead and hum a tune. I'm going outdoors for a while."

He laughed as he pushed himself up. "I'll join you. Shall we saddle the horses and go for a short ride before I have to go home?"

She frowned and shook her head. "I want to be alone! Go find Ben. You came to see him."

He shook his head. "I came to see you."

Her eyes widened and she swallowed hard. "To tease me?"

"Me? Tease Libby Dobbs?"

She squared her shoulders and glared at him. "See? You always do!" She marched past him toward the wide doorway, but he caught her arm as she reached the door. She tried to get away, but he turned her so she had to face him. Finally she looked up, meeting his angry gaze.

"I want you to forget about Scott Norris. He's too old for you. You need to use your time and energy for piano instead of mooning over Scott Norris."

"What I do or don't do is none of your business!"

"I'll make it my business," he said in a low, tense voice.

44

She felt his grip loosen and she twisted free. "Leave me alone, Jerry Grosbeck! I don't have time for you!" For a minute she thought she'd hurt his feelings, but then he laughed and she knew she'd been wrong.

"See you in church tomorrow, Libby. Save me a seat."

She ran from the family room, but his laugh followed her. She grabbed her jacket off the back porch and slipped it on as she pushed her way outdoors. The cold wind cooled her burning cheeks, and she thankfully greeted Rex as he barked a welcome and pushed his black and tan head against her hand.

"Oh, Rex, I'll be so glad when Jerry leaves! I think he's terrible! I don't want him to come here ever again!" A slight sound behind her made her turn. Jerry stood there and she knew he'd heard what she'd said by the hurt look on his face. He just stared at her, then hurried past to his ten-speed and cycled quickly down the long drive to the road.

Elizabeth sniffed hard, then wiped the hot tears off her cheeks. Why should she feel bad? He deserved to have his feelings hurt for the times he'd teased her. She wouldn't give Jerry Grosbeck another thought! She'd think about Scott Norris and only him.

Six
The missing love letters

Elizabeth tucked her hands behind her head and lay back on her pillow as she watched the path the sun made across her room. She remembered the first time she'd seen this room when she was eleven and had just been brought to the Johnson farm by Miss Miller. The room had been more beautiful than any room she'd ever seen. Other bedrooms she'd lived in had been painted in dull tones with shabby furniture. But this room was red and dark pink and a lighter pink, and the furniture was new and beautiful. A big pink dog had sat on the bed and Vera had said that Susan had given it for a welcoming gift.

With a smile Elizabeth looked at Pinky who wasn't nearly as fluffy and bright as he had been then. Often she'd pressed her face against him and sobbed, leaving tearstains behind. He hadn't minded a bit, and she'd always felt much better.

The last time Rhonda Lincoln had stayed with them, Elizabeth had cried many times against Pinky.

She squirmed restlessly. How would Rhonda act now that she was eighteen years old and happy with her parents? Would she try to be the big boss this time? Well, she'd better stay away from Snowball!

Elizabeth sat up and pulled her knees up under her chin. Rhonda had sure taken over Snowball's training when she was here last and now that Snowball was trained, she wouldn't have any reason to be around her. But what if Rhonda preferred riding Snowball? Would Dad let her have her own way? But maybe Rhonda didn't like horses anymore. With Uncle Steve and Aunt Ellen here, maybe Rhonda wouldn't be such a hotshot.

"Forget Rhonda," muttered Elizabeth as she swung her long legs over the edge of the bed. She rubbed her hands over her nightgown with a sigh. She would not allow Rhonda to take away the excitement of Thanksgiving. Scott was coming, and that was the best news possible.

"Scott!" She stared at her desk. How could she have forgotten to check on the love letters yesterday? She quivered as she walked to the desk. She gulped, then whisked open the drawer and reached in for the folder of love letters. Her hand touched wood and she dropped to her knees and peered into the drawer.

The folder was gone!

The love letters were gone!

She bit back a cry of anguish, then jerked open one drawer at a time and searched carefully.

The love letters were missing!

With a plop she landed on the floor, her hand trembling at her mouth, her hazel eyes wide. Her heartbeats sounded loud in the quiet room.

Who had taken the letters? How could she ask anyone without giving away her secret?

Tears of frustration sprang to her eyes and she wanted to howl in pain the way an animal would.

Had Toby and Jacob taken them?

With a ragged sob she pushed herself up. She'd march to Toby's room right now and find out if he had the folder of letters. But she'd have to be careful what she said so that if he hadn't taken them he wouldn't guess what was missing.

The house was quiet and she knew Mom and Dad would be up before long to get chores done before Sunday school and church.

She stopped outside Toby's door. It was open a crack and she could hear him snoring. She clenched her fists at her sides and narrowed her eyes. How could he just lie there and snore?

Stealthily she crept into the blue room, then looked around quickly for a yellow folder. She frowned. It wouldn't be in sight. He'd have hidden it, or worse given it to Jacob to take home. Her heart sank to her bare feet and she felt glued to the spot. Oh, she had to find that folder!

Toby turned and his arm flung out almost over the edge of the bed. Elizabeth wanted to jerk him out of bed and demand to know if he'd taken the folder of letters, but she stood still and he didn't awaken.

As silently as she could, she looked through his desk and dresser, then his closet. She bumped against a model plane that was half built and it fell to the floor. She lifted her foot to smash it, then hesitated. The old Libby Dobbs would have done it, but she couldn't. She was a Christian, learning to be like Jesus.

Slowly she stepped away from the plane and walked from the room, her shoulders drooping. Sometimes it was easy to be Christlike; other times it was very hard.

She sank to the edge of her unmade bed and locked her long fingers together. Since the folder wasn't in Toby's room, where was it? He wouldn't have had Jacob take the letters home. Not Toby. He'd keep them and tease her about them, and maybe send them to Scott.

She leaped up in panic. What could she do?

Once again she rushed down the quiet hall and into Toby's room. She shook him awake and he sat up, his red hair mussed and his freckles standing boldly out against his suddenly pale face.

"What's wrong, Elizabeth? You're scaring me."

"Toby, there's a yellow folder that had letters in it missing from my desk drawer. Did you or Jacob take it?" She wanted to shake the truth from him, but she forced herself to stand over him as calmly as possible.

Toby frowned and shook his head. "We didn't take anything, We were looking at your puzzle box and that's all! Honest. Why would we want to take a folder of letters?"

She knew by his face that he was telling the truth. Angry tears burned her eyes. "Then who did take the folder? Who was in my room?"

Toby shrugged. "I saw Jerry Grosbeck in there yesterday."

"Jerry!" She quickly lowered her voice. "Why would he go into my room?"

"He said he just wanted to see it," said Toby with a shrug.

Sure, he did. And he'd love to find those love letters and then make sure everyone else saw them, including Scott.

She whipped around and rushed to her room, her chest rising and falling, her fists balled at her sides.

Jerry Grosbeck! She should've known he was the one! He probably was getting even with her for keeping his dad's war medal all those years. She had finally given it back, but maybe he was still mad.

She flushed painfully as she thought about Jerry sitting down to read the letters to Scott. Would Jerry laugh at what she wrote? Would he make fun of her?

She forced herself to slip on her jeans and sweatshirt so she could do her outdoor chores before breakfast. How could she face her family without their guessing how upset she was?

Downstairs she forced out a bright "Good morning" to Chuck and Vera, then hurried to the back porch for her jacket and boots.

"I want to stay home today," Susan said behind Elizabeth.

She looked over her thin shoulder. "Why?"

Susan rolled her eyes and sighed. "You

should know. Joe!" She jerked on her tan jacket and zipped it up roughly. "Stay with me today, Elizabeth. Please. Don't let Joe near me!"

Elizabeth frowned impatiently. Didn't Susan know she had problems of her own? "Grow up, Susan! You don't have to be afraid of seeing Joe. What can he do to you? He wants to go with other girls and let you go with other boys. What's the big deal?"

Susan rammed her hat down on her bright head. "I might have known you wouldn't understand! You're so busy with the piano, you don't know the first thing about love!" She rushed out the door, but Elizabeth caught it before it slammed shut.

Cold air blew against her in the yard as she stood staring after Susan. What would Susan say if she knew about Scott? Did Susan think she had the only heart in the Johnson family?

Rex barked and tugged against his chain. Elizabeth wanted to unhook him, but she knew he had to stay chained until they came back from church. A horse nickered from inside the barn, and Elizabeth knew Snowball was anxious to have breakfast and to be let out into the pen beside the barn.

For once she didn't take time to talk to Snowball or the other horses as she fed

them and turned them out. Snowball
nuzzled her neck, but she pushed her away.

Jerry probably couldn't wait to get to
church so that he could see her and tease
her about the love letters. He'd probably
stand outside the Sunday school wing and
wait. He might even wave one of the letters
over his head and roar with laughter.

"He'll be very, very sorry," she muttered
as she ran to the house. She pushed past
Ben on the back porch and he asked her
what was wrong, but she ignored him.

At the breakfast table Elizabeth pushed
the egg Vera had fried for her around and
around on the plate. It was impossible to
even think about eating at a time like this!
She forced down a small glass of orange
juice. Voices buzzed around her head, but
she didn't hear what the others were saying.
Finally she pushed back her chair and
excused herself. Chuck caught her arm as
she walked past him.

"Is there anything that I can help you
with, Elizabeth?" he asked in a low voice
for her ears alone.

Tears pricked her eyes as she shook her
head.

"I love you, and I'm always here if you
want to talk."

"Thanks," she whispered hoarsely.

He winked and released her and she

reluctantly walked away. Maybe he could help her. Maybe he could shake the letters right out of Jerry.

By the time they reached the church, her throat was too tight to speak. She stopped cold at the sight of Jerry standing beside the back door of the church. Kevin bumped into her.

"You forgot to signal, Elizabeth," he said with a laugh.

"Close it!" she snapped as she glared at him. She saw the pain and surprise but turned around and slowly, deliberately walked toward Jerry.

"Hi, Jerry," said Ben. "Are you waiting for me?"

"For me," said Elizabeth sharply as she caught Jerry's arm tightly.

"Hey, what's this?" He laughed and because he looked as if he were enjoying the extra attention from her, her anger rose.

"I want to talk to you alone right now," she hissed just above a whisper.

"I'm all yours," he said with a nervous laugh. "What got you so mad? What did I do this time? Don't tell me you're still angry about that kiss."

She wanted to knock him down in the grass next to the sidewalk, but she just stood there and looked at him. She waited until several people walked past before she said, "Where are my letters?"

He frowned and she was amazed that he could act so puzzled. Was it an act, or didn't he know about the letters?

"My letters, Jerry!" She shook his arm.

"People are looking at us, Libby. Who knows what they might think." His dark eyes twinkled and she dropped his arm as if it had burned her.

"I want my letters back right now! Do you hear me?"

"I don't know what you're talking about."

She stamped her booted foot. "You were in my room yesterday. Toby saw you." She saw the flush creep up over his face and ears. "So! You remember!"

He ducked his head, then looked at her. "I was in your room. So what? I just looked around. I remember that terrible room you had when we stayed with the Adairs. I am happy for you now. Your room is beautiful. And it's just what you deserve."

She blinked in surprise.

"Shall we go in now?" He lifted his dark brows and she could only nod.

She walked inside with him, and then as he walked to join Ben she realized she still didn't know if he had the letters.

She had to get them back before Scott read them! She sat down in the back corner of the Sunday school room and locked her icy hands together.

Seven
Thanksgiving

Elizabeth hooked her fingers behind her
back and paced back and forth across her
bedroom. Why couldn't she just hide in
her room for the rest of the week? How
could she face Scott, not knowing if he'd
read the letters?

She closed her eyes and whimpered.
Why had she written those letters? She
should have kept the thoughts and feelings
to herself, and not written them down. If
only she knew who had taken the letters so
that she could figure out what to do next!

Yesterday coming home on the bus Jill
had asked her if anything was wrong, but
she'd shrugged it away. She couldn't talk
about it aloud, not even to Jill. It really was
too awful to think about, but the thoughts
pressed against her mind and wouldn't
leave her.

Someone knocked and she jumped in alarm. Was Scott here already? He planned on coming about eleven. Maybe he was early. How could she face him?

"Libby, open the door!"

It was Susan. Elizabeth exhaled in relief as she unlocked her door and opened it, and Susan rushed in, her face glowing.

"Oh, Libby! The most exciting thing happened to me!"

Elizabeth sat carefully on the edge of her bed as she wondered if she wanted to hear Susan's news.

Susan flipped her long red-gold hair back and stood with her hands on her narrow waist. She was dressed in her new blue slacks and lighter blue sweater. "I am finally over Joe!" She waited and Elizabeth wondered if she was expected to shout or jump up and down. Susan frowned with her head tilted. "Don't you understand? My heart isn't broken now. I feel wonderful!" She twirled around with a happy laugh, then sank down on the hassock.

"I thought you'd love Joe forever," said Elizabeth dryly.

Susan wrinkled her small nose. "I know. But I was wrong. I am in love with someone much nicer and better looking and taller and everything!"

Elizabeth knew she was expected to ask who. "Who is he, Susan?"

Susan hugged herself and her blue eyes sparkled. "Jerry Grosbeck!"

Elizabeth sat absolutely still. She felt as if the breath had been knocked out of her body. Jerry Grosbeck? "But—but I thought you didn't like him at all. You said a lot of things about him—all bad."

"I changed my mind." She sighed a long, deep sigh. "I've been talking to him a lot lately, and he's very interesting to talk to. A lot of the girls in our class like him."

Elizabeth swallowed hard and suddenly felt as if she were going to cry. "I didn't know that."

"They think the scar on his face is very romantic."

"Romantic?" Elizabeth jumped up. "How can it be romantic? It was a terrible thing to have happen."

"I know, but it makes him different from the other boys." Susan rubbed her hands up and down her arms. "I am going to make sure he asks me to go with him."

"You wouldn't!"

Susan frowned and stood up. "Why should that upset you? Just because you don't like him much doesn't mean I can't."

Elizabeth gnawed the inside of her bottom lip as she stared down at the carpet. Why should she care if Susan went with Jerry? Maybe he'd stop teasing her and acting so funny.

58

"Are you going downstairs now, Libby? Uncle Steve will be here soon, and then Scott."

"Yes. Yes, I'll go down with you." Being with Susan would be much easier than walking into a room where company already sat, especially if Scott were there. She'd have to sit quietly in a corner and watch his face to know if he'd read her letters. But maybe whoever took them hadn't sent them to Scott. Maybe the culprit was waiting to show the letters to Scott while he was here!

Elizabeth stumbled and had to grab the banister to stop herself from pitching down the stairs. What would she do if she were forced to watch Scott read her love letters to him? She leaned weakly against the newel post while the grandfather clock steadily tick-ticked away.

"Elizabeth, are you ill?" asked Vera in concern, squeezing Elizabeth's shoulder.

She looked at Vera and wanted to fling her arms around her and bury her face in Vera's neck. "I'm all right."

"Honey, I wish you'd tell me what's been upsetting you for the past few days. I might be able to help."

Elizabeth shook her head and managed a weak smile. "Has anyone come yet?"

"Not yet, but they'll be here before long, I'm sure." Vera studied Elizabeth thoughtfully. "Don't forget that whatever problem, whatever heartache you have, you have a heavenly Father who loves you very much and will help you. Never try to handle things without his help."

Elizabeth sniffed and nodded, thankful to hear Vera's words. She watched Vera walk away, her cranberry skirts swishing around her legs. The scent of her perfume lingered in the air for a minute, then was over-powered by the aroma of turkey and dressing.

Elizabeth stopped in the doorway of the family room, and Ben looked up from the book he was reading.

"Come play for me, Elizabeth." He closed his book and smiled and she wanted to run to him and hug him. He always made her feel good.

"What shall I play?"

"Whatever you want." He crossed his long legs at the ankles and smiled at her. He was dressed in brown cords and a tan sweater shirt. His red hair was combed neatly for now. She knew his habit of running his fingers through his hair when he was in deep thought.

"I'm glad you're my brother, Ben," she said in a voice which broke. She wanted to tell him just how much he meant to her, but she didn't want to burst into tears.

A strange look crossed his face and he

shrugged. "I hope you always feel that way. I don't want the famous concert pianist to forget she had a brother named Ben."

She laughed as she sat at the piano. "I will never forget!"

"And you will be famous! Nothing will stop you!"

She looked quickly over her shoulder at him. Why did he sound so fervent? He should know that nothing would keep her from becoming a concert pianist. "It'll help if I win the competition next month."

"You'll win!"

Her eyes widened and he grinned sheepishly.

"I get carried away, Elizabeth. I know how much your career means to you. It means a lot to me, too. I want you to succeed as much as you want to. But right now I want to hear you play."

She opened her book and touched her fingers to the keys. She'd drown herself in the music and forget her problems for now. She closed her eyes and silently asked the Lord to give her an answer to her problem; then she played for Ben and for herself. Finally when she stopped playing, she turned to smile at Ben and found the room full. Everyone clapped and she gasped, then looked right into Scott's blue eyes. She wanted to sink out of sight, but he smiled at her as if he were happy to see her. If he'd read her letters he wouldn't be smiling that way, would he?

"You play beautifully, Elizabeth," said Aunt Ellen from where she stood beside Vera. "We've heard good reports, but listening to you is even better than we'd imagined."

"Thank you." Elizabeth finally looked from Aunt Ellen to Uncle Steve, who had the same blond coloring as Vera, then to Rhonda. But Rhonda wasn't looking toward the piano. She was looking at Scott and Elizabeth could tell Rhonda liked what she saw. Elizabeth clenched her teeth.

"Our girl has special talent," said Chuck as he slipped his arm around Elizabeth's shoulders. "She'll play for you again before the weekend is over."

"I want to hear more about the competition that's coming," said Scott.

"What do you want to know?" Did she sound breathless? Why couldn't she gather her thoughts so she could talk with Scott instead of just standing and looking at him?

Before Scott could speak, Rhonda stepped forward with a bright smile. "I've heard a gospel song lately written by a man named Scott Norris. Is that you, or are there two of you?" When she smiled at him that way, she looked breathtakingly beautiful and Elizabeth glanced quickly at Scott. An icy band tightened around her heart at the look on Scott's face.

What if he fell in love with Rhonda Lincoln? Elizabeth wanted to grab Scott and rush him from the room as he talked to Rhonda about the music that he wrote and the songs he'd had published.

Elizabeth's legs buckled and she plopped onto the piano bench, her elbow striking a key. Rhonda looked at her knowingly and she felt sick. Did Rhonda guess her secret love for Scott? Elizabeth shuddered. Had she given it away by the way she'd looked at Scott? Oh, how awful! She glanced at Ben where he sat on the floor near the couch. He looked from her to Scott, then to Rhonda. What was Ben thinking?

"Rhonda. Scott. Please have a chair," said Chuck from his place on the couch beside Vera and Ellen. Steve sat on the arm of the couch with his arm around Ellen, and Elizabeth remembered how close they'd come to being divorced two years ago.

"I guess I get carried away when I talk about my music," said Scott with a laugh. "Elizabeth and I have a lot in common."

She flushed and managed a weak smile, but she made sure she kept her eyes off Scott.

"I want to get better acquainted, Scott," said Rhonda with a shake of her blonde hair. "I've never met a songwriter before. Could we go for a walk and talk?"

Scott smiled and quickly agreed. He seemed to want to be alone with Rhonda as badly as she wanted to be alone with him. Elizabeth wanted to push Rhonda aside and walk with Scott herself, but she stayed on the piano bench with her hands locked tightly together. Rhonda's laugh floated back. The day suddenly seemed dull and gray to Elizabeth. Would the whole weekend be like this?

Eight
Scott

Elizabeth peeked at Scott, sitting at Ben's side across the table, then looked quickly down at the slice of turkey on her plate. How could she eat Thanksgiving dinner with Scott at the same table? She forced herself to taste the cranberry salad, then realized that she was very hungry. She listened to the chatter and the clink of forks on the china plates as she ate the hot rolls with melted butter dripping from them, turkey and dressing with cranberry sauce, mashed potatoes with turkey gravy, and the fruit salad that she'd made by herself last night. She was glad that she had sat between Susan and Kevin and didn't have to talk to Rhonda. That would really ruin her appetite!

"Would anyone care for pumpkin pie with whipped cream now?" asked Vera with a smile.

Elizabeth added her groan to the others.

"Let's wait until later," said Chuck as he pushed back his chair. "We'll clear off the table and then I want to show Steve around the farm."

"I need a walk after that delicious meal," said Steve with a grin. "I need a *long* walk!"

"I want to see Snowball," said Rhonda in a bright voice, and Elizabeth almost dropped the silverware in her hands.

Elizabeth darted a look at Rhonda, but she was looking at Scott. Elizabeth's knuckles turned white from gripping the silverware tightly. She knew Rhonda wanted Scott to go for another walk with her, and she was really rubbing it in by wanting to see Snowball.

"We could go for a ride," said Rhonda as she moved out of the way of Toby as he reached for the plate that had held the cranberry salad.

Scott turned to Ben. "Why don't you take Rhonda for a ride since she wants to see Snowball. I want to talk to Elizabeth."

Her heart leaped, then dropped at the determined look on Rhonda's face. Rhonda wasn't going to go with Ben willingly.

Elizabeth turned to Ben and mouthed for him to take Rhonda, but he turned away almost angrily and said, "You go ahead with her, Scott. You can always talk to Elizabeth, but you can't ride after dark."

"Please, Scott," said Rhonda with a little pout. Then she turned to Elizabeth. "You won't mind me riding Snowball, will you? You know how good I am with her."

Elizabeth did mind, but she knew it wouldn't make any difference to Rhonda. Elizabeth shrugged and hurried to the kitchen. Rhonda couldn't possibly keep Scott occupied all the time, could she?

In the kitchen she dropped the silverware in the container of the dishwasher, waited a few minutes while Vera and Ellen talked and laughed, then walked back to the dining room. She nudged Ben and frowned. "Why didn't you go with Rhonda?" she whispered sharply.

Ben shrugged. "I didn't want to."

"But you knew *I* wanted you to."

He frowned and pushed his hands deep into his pockets. "And do you always get what you want?"

She backed away, her eyes wide in surprise. Ben was usually very nice to her. What was wrong with him? Did he hate riding with Rhonda?

Ben picked up the last dish off the table and carried it to the kitchen. Slowly Elizabeth folded the tablecloth and took it outside to shake off the crumbs. She wouldn't think about Rhonda riding Snowball with Scott beside her on Apache Girl.

"Libby, play Ping-Pong with me, will you?" asked Susan as Elizabeth walked into the family room later.

Elizabeth hesitated, then agreed. She looked longingly at the piano, then followed Susan to the basement.

"I'm going to invite Jerry over for tomorrow," said Susan as she picked up the blue paddle.

Elizabeth gripped the red paddle. "Why? Who wants him here?"

Susan laughed and raised her eyebrows. "I do."

"He won't come."

"Oh, yes, he will."

Elizabeth wanted to fling the paddle away and run upstairs away from Susan. "You think every boy around will fall for you. You think all you have to do is call Jerry and he'll come running."

"Why are you mad?" Susan stood with her hands on her hips. "I sure can't understand you."

Elizabeth ducked her head. She didn't understand herself. Finally she picked up the small white ball. "Shall we volley for serve?"

Susan hesitated, then grinned and nodded.

Just as Susan beat her for the third time, Scott walked down the steps and stood beside the fireplace. "I'll play you next, Elizabeth."

68

She laughed breathlessly as she darted a look for Rhonda. She was nowhere in sight. Now, if Susan would leave, she could be alone with Scott! Finally Susan excused herself and ran upstairs.

"Do you really want to play?" asked Elizabeth. Was her hair still curly and pretty? Did she have a smudge of dirt on her face or were her clothes messed up at all? How she wanted to look just right for Scott!

He motioned for her to sit down on the rug near the fireplace. She joined him and suddenly bubbled with happiness.

Scott smiled at Elizabeth. "Tell me how you've been. Your letters are so short I can't tell what's happening with you."

She flushed as she thought of the missing love letters. They were not short at all! "Mostly I've been practicing for the competition that I told you about." She talked for a while about that and then asked him about his music.

"I have a song that I'm working on now. Brian Taylor is arranging it for me and the group Servant is going to sing it in concert soon." Scott told her more about his work and how happy he was now. "And my family is coming around. They like my music, but they're still surprised that I want to make it my occupation."

"I bet they're really very proud of you."

69

She wanted to hold his hand or lean against him. She pulled her knees up to her chin and wrapped her arms around her legs as she watched his face.

"You never told me about your cousin Rhonda before."

She froze at the strange inflection in his voice as he said Rhonda's name. "I told you she was coming today with her parents."

"I guess I expected a little girl. How old is she?"

"Eighteen." Why did he want to talk about Rhonda?

He brushed a hair off his sleeve. "Does she have a boyfriend?"

"Who knows? If she does we never heard about him."

"She's beautiful, and she likes my music."

"Yeah."

"She's a lot like your mother."

Elizabeth's eyes widened. How could spoiled Rhonda be like Vera? "In what way?" My, but it was hard to keep her voice normal!

"She loves kids. She's studying to be a kindergarten teacher."

"Rhonda is?"

Scott lifted an eyebrow. "Why are you surprised?"

"Maybe I don't know Rhonda."

"She told me about training Snowball for

70

you when she stayed here for a while. She said you couldn't handle Snowball as firmly as she needed to be handled."

Elizabeth squirmed restlessly. "Rhonda did a good job with Snowball. I guess I just wanted to do it myself."

"I admire you for standing back so she could do it since she was better at it."

"Dad made me."

"Oh."

Why hadn't she kept her big mouth closed? Couldn't she let him admire her for something?

"I'm taking Rhonda to town tonight for a while."

Elizabeth's heart sank and she wanted to bury her head in her arms and sob. Why hadn't Rhonda stayed away?

Scott pushed himself up and sat on the edge of an ottoman. "Your piano playing has improved even since summer, Elizabeth. You must practice a lot."

"I do, but I love it."

He nodded. "I know what you mean. I get lost in my music and a whole afternoon is gone before I realize it."

"Susan can't understand at all. I don't know about the others."

"Susan probably is too busy with boyfriends to think of piano. She's a pretty little thing and smart, too."

"All she ever thinks about is boys."

Elizabeth twisted a curl around and around her finger. "Now she thinks she's in love with . . . Jerry Grosbeck. She really thinks she is!"

"And what about you, Elizabeth? Do you find any time for a boyfriend?"

Dare she tell him that he was the only boyfriend that she would ever want? Oh, no! She couldn't embarrass herself again with Scott. "I'm too busy with piano to think about boys." Scott was a man, not a boy.

"I've gone out with a couple of girls, but nothing serious." He sighed. "But Rhonda is different. I wish we lived closer so we could really get to know each other."

Elizabeth jumped up and forced a bright smile. "I think its time for pumpkin pie or apple pie or whatever pie you want, don't you?"

Scott grinned as he stood up. "I didn't think I'd want to look at food again, but pie sounds delicious. Lead the way, my friend."

She walked with him and joined the others in the dining room. Her heart sank as he quickly found a chair next to Rhonda.

Her taste for pie was suddenly gone. Elizabeth quietly walked to the family room and sat at the piano, her head down, tears pricking her eyes.

Nine
A broken heart

Elizabeth opened the barn door to step out, then gasped and quickly closed it again. Susan really had called Jerry Grosbeck and he'd actually come! He was smiling at Susan as if he were very glad to see her! Oh, she didn't want to see Jerry. She didn't want to see anybody!

She couldn't stay in the barn all Friday afternoon, could she? She looked toward the back door, then nodded firmly. She'd sneak around the barn and slip into the house without Jerry or Susan seeing her. That's just what she'd do. And if Jerry tried to find her in the barn, he'd be out of luck.

Maybe he wouldn't look for her. Maybe he wouldn't remember that she existed with Susan around—Susan with her "Miss Teenage America" body and her great love for Jerry.

Elizabeth shivered. She knew it wasn't

from the cold, but couldn't understand why. And right now she wouldn't take the time to think about her actions or reactions or feelings or anything. She had to get to the house before Jerry saw her.

Cautiously she crept around the end of the barn, then peeked out. Susan and Jerry stood facing the house with their backs to her. She dashed to a nearby oak and hid behind it. Was Elizabeth Gail Johnson, concert pianist, really doing this? She bit her lip to keep from laughing aloud.

Goosy Poosy honked from inside the chicken pen where Chuck had insisted Toby lock him until company left on Sunday. Goosy Poosy was always friendly to the family he knew, but lately he'd been biting people he didn't know. Rhonda had said she certainly didn't want to take a chance on the goose knocking her down and flapping his wide wings against her.

Elizabeth carefully peeked around the tree, then dashed to another tree, this one closer to the cow barn. Why didn't Susan take Jerry inside?

Rex barked in the distance. Elizabeth knew Toby and Kevin had taken him on a hike with them. If he'd been home, he'd have given her away for sure.

She slipped behind a clump of birch, then stopped in alarm. Scott and Rhonda were walking around the cow barn and coming right toward her. What should she do? If she stepped out, Susan and Jerry would see her. If she stayed there, Scott and Rhonda would see her and think she was spying on them. She looked frantically around, chewing her lip thoughtfully.

Just then the back door of the house slammed and Elizabeth was sure Susan had finally taken Jerry inside. Now she could step out and greet Scott and Rhonda, then race to the house and to her room where she could hide until Jerry left.

She started to take a step when she heard Scott say, "Rhonda, it seems as if we've known each other forever, doesn't it?"

Elizabeth couldn't move. Maybe they'd walk right past and not notice her. But they stopped near another tree so that she was completely hidden from them. She could hear them as if she were beside them and her face burned. She dare not stay here, but if she moved now they'd think for sure she was spying. She pressed her hand to her mouth in despair.

"Scott, I knew the minute I saw you that you'd be special to me," Rhonda said tenderly.

"I knew, too," Scott said, then they laughed softly together. "I don't think we hid our feelings very well."

"Libby was jealous," Rhonda said sharply.

Elizabeth wanted to die on the spot.

Scott chuckled. "Why would she be jealous? She's a little kid yet."

"Little kids get ideas, too, and she can easily fall for a good-looking guy like you who pays attention to her."

Elizabeth tugged at her too tight jacket. How could Scott talk about her to Rhonda?

"I like Elizabeth," said Scott, and Elizabeth lifted her pointed chin high. "Right now I want to talk about us, Rhonda. We can't lose track of each other now that we've found each other. I'm falling in love with you, Rhonda."

"I'm falling in love with you, too, Scott," said Rhonda softly.

Elizabeth fought against the tears threatening to gush down her cheeks. She would not cry and make noise! Carefully she peeked through the branches. Her eyes widened as she saw Scott pull Rhonda close and kiss her. Oh! How could he kiss Rhonda? How could he love her?

Finally Scott said, "We could see about your transferring to the college near me. Please think about it. Is it asking too much too soon?"

Rhonda was quiet so long that Elizabeth peeked out again, only to snap her eyes shut in pain. Once again Rhonda was in Scott's arms. The idea of seeing Scott often seemed to appeal to her. Elizabeth wanted

76

to rush out and jerk out Rhonda's long blonde hair, then knock her to the cold ground. But what good would it do? Scott would only pick her up and kiss her again.

Finally Scott and Rhonda walked away and Elizabeth sighed in relief. Now, she could get to her room and cry against Pinky all she wanted. She turned to run back to the first oak near the horse barn, then froze in her tracks. Jerry Grosbeck stood there looking at her. With a muffled cry she sprang away, but he was after her and caught her immediately.

"Did you take to spying now, Libby? It's not enough that you fell for an old man, but now you have to spy on him and his girlfriend."

"Let me go!" She twisted and turned and tried to jerk free. How dare he grab her! How dare he spy on her! "I hate you, Jerry Grosbeck!"

"It looks like all those love letters you wrote to Scott didn't do any good."

She gasped and stared speechlessly at him. He *had* taken the letters! But would he show them to Scott? She'd die if Scott saw them now after what he'd said about her being a kid!

"I'd sure like to read the letters he wrote to you. He probably thought it was fun to write love letters to a girl like you while he waited for one his own age."

77

"I want my letters!" she whispered hoarsely.

"Sure you do. You want to keep them locked away to read for the rest of your life so you won't really have to fall in love. You can just dream about it. You're a good one for that."

"Let me go, Jerry! Please! Go back to Susan. She wants you." Elizabeth struggled again, but his grip tightened and finally she stopped and looked at him questioningly.

"Scott has probably read your letters over and over just like you read his. What would he do if Rhonda read them? Maybe she wouldn't be so ready to fall all over him."

"Don't, Jerry!" Elizabeth fought against the humiliating tears. "Don't show the letters to anyone else. Please."

He frowned. "What are you talking about? Why would I show your love letters around?"

Her hazel eyes grew round in surprise. "You won't show them to anyone? You honestly won't?"

He shook her a little. "How can I when you have his letters and he has yours?"

Her throat almost closed and her mind whirled with crazy thoughts. Was Jerry saying that he didn't have the yellow folder of love letters? Maybe he didn't know anything about that folder!

"What's wrong, Libby? You look like you're going to faint or something. I'm sorry if I upset you. I know you're hurt because of that Scott Norris, and I shouldn't have yelled at you."

Tears slowly filled her eyes and she turned quickly to hide them. Why should his soft, kind words make her cry? What was wrong with her?

He cleared his throat and stood awkwardly beside her, and finally she gained control of herself again.

If he didn't have the missing letters, then who did?

Just then Susan called Jerry. He hesitated, then said to Elizabeth, "I have to see what she wants. I'll talk to you later."

She nodded, then watched him run toward Susan who loved him and wanted to go with him.

Why did Susan always get her way? Elizabeth knuckled away the remaining tears impatiently. She loved Scott, but he loved Rhonda. What a terrible, terrible vacation this was turning out to be! Thanksgiving was ruined. Everything was ruined!

Slowly she walked toward the house with her head down. She stopped beside the picnic table and remembered the cookout they'd had last summer with Scott. She'd sat beside him and she'd been happy. Would she ever be happy again?

Finally she walked to the back door. As she reached to open it, Scott called to her. She froze, then slowly turned around to wait for Scott and Rhonda to reach her. They both looked happy. Did they know that she was ready to burst into tears?

"Elizabeth, would you have time to play for us?" asked Scott with a wide smile, a smile that she would have thought was full of love earlier.

She looked at her hands with a scowl. Could she play for them? Could she ever play the piano again when her heart was broken?

"Libby, you're shaking with cold," said Rhonda in concern. "Let's get you inside and get you warm so we can hear your beautiful music."

Elizabeth slowly walked inside. Sure, Rhonda could be as nice as anything now that she had what she wanted.

"I'll take your jacket so you can go in by the fire and warm yourself," said Scott as he pulled her arm free. His touch burned her and she jerked away and hung up her own jacket right beside Chuck's old red plaid farm coat.

She turned to Scott, but couldn't lift her eyes past the buttons on his shirt. "I don't feel like playing now. I'm going to my room."

Scott caught her hand and she lifted

startled eyes to his. "Did I hear you correctly? Elizabeth Gail Johnson, concert pianist, doesn't feel like playing? Is something wrong?"

She could name a few things, but she carefully pulled free and walked away.

"Play for us later," Rhonda called after her.

Elizabeth reached the stairs, then ran up two at a time. In her room she flung herself down on her bed and buried her face against Pinky. Her life was over. Nothing mattered anymore.

Ten
The mystery solved

Elizabeth turned from her bedroom window with her lips pressed tightly together. She would not spend all of Saturday in her bedroom hiding away from Scott! She would find the love letters even if she had to search the entire house, so that whoever took them couldn't show them to Scott! She should have looked before until she found them. She shouldn't have hidden away because of the letters or because Scott loved Rhonda.

Elizabeth frowned as she absently rubbed the soft sleeve of her flowered shirt. Where should she look first? Maybe she should start in the room next to hers and work her way around all the bedrooms before she started looking downstairs.

She opened her door and hesitated. She knew Toby was playing with Jacob and

Kevin with Paul. Susan was expecting Jerry any minute and Ben had been outdoors the last she knew.

The faint scent of Aunt Ellen's perfume hung in the air as Elizabeth walked to Susan's room. Susan would be very angry if she caught her. And she'd tell Mom and Dad for sure. Elizabeth hesitated, then opened the door and walked in. She had to find the yellow folder of letters!

Carefully she locked Susan's door so she wouldn't be surprised by anyone, then systematically began searching the dresser, chest, desk, and closet. She even looked under the bed, but the yellow folder wasn't there.

"I'm glad Susan didn't take it," she whispered as she absently fingered a pad of paper on the desk. Then she looked at the pad. Susan had written "Susan-n-Jerry forever."

Elizabeth swallowed hard and stepped away from the desk before she ripped the page off the pad and crumpled it up into a small, tight ball. How could Susan think she'd love Jerry forever? She'd said she would love Joe forever.

Elizabeth rushed to the door and out into the hallway. She didn't want to look at that note again. She'd check Toby's room again, then Kevin's. She dared not look in the guestrooms or her parents'.

Quickly but thoroughly she looked in Toby's room, then in Kevin's. She frowned as she picked up the booklet on detective procedures. Maybe she should become a detective along with Kevin so that she could find the missing love letters.

At Ben's door she hesitated. How could she look in Ben's room? She knew he would never take anything from her room. Ben never did anything bad. She sighed unhappily as she reached for the doorknob. She had to look or she'd never be satisified.

The knob turned silently and she pushed open the door just as silently. Her eyes widened and she almost closed the door again. Ben was inside at his desk with his back to her. How could she explain to him why she'd walked into his room without knocking? As she hesitated Ben stood up and turned around. In his hands was the yellow folder!

"Ben!"

Quickly he hid the folder behind his back, his eyes wide in alarm and his face red with embarrassment.

"Ben, you took my letters!" She couldn't comprehend it. Ben would never do such a thing.

"How could you write letters like this?"

She doubled her fists. "How could you walk into my room and take my folder of letters? Why did you do it?"

"Lower your voice or everyone in the house will be up here to see why you're yelling. And you wouldn't want Scott embarrassed like that, would you?" Ben laughed dryly as he looked down at the letters. His red hair was on end and his face a sick shade of gray.

"I want my letters, Ben." She walked toward him and he stood his ground, his eyes boring into hers. "Did you show them to—to Scott?"

"I thought about it."

She reached for the folder but he held it out of her reach. "Why are you doing this to me, Ben? Why?"

His hazel eyes looked shiny as if he were about to cry. "Do you know how much time and energy you waste on Scott Norris? You should be thinking about your piano and not him!"

She frowned. "But I *do* think about piano! I don't give up my practice time to write to him."

"Oh, sure. You never sit and daydream about him or anything, do you? You never hide away in your room and write to him, do you?"

She flushed guiltily.

"You are a concert pianist! You don't have time for Scott Norris!"

She slumped to the edge of Ben's bed and he dropped down on his chair next to his desk. "Ben, I don't know what to say. I can't understand why you're treating me this way."

He pushed his fingers through his hair. "Elizabeth, I'm only trying to help you accomplish your dream. I don't want anything to stand in your way."

"Nothing is!"

"Scott Norris might be. He is taking more and more of your time, and I don't like it."

"Ben!" She leaped up, her eyes blazing. "It's not your business! I can love Scott all I want! I can write to him all I want!"

Ben clutched the folder so tightly it folded. "If you do, then I'll show these letters to Scott."

"You wouldn't dare!" She wanted to leap on Ben and grab the folder, but she knew he was much stronger than she. She'd die if he showed Scott the letters!

"I will, Elizabeth, unless you forget him. He's too old for you anyway and now he's falling for Rhonda."

"You wouldn't really do it, would you, Ben?" She could barely keep the tears back. How could she trust Ben again?

He rubbed his hand down his jeans. "I don't want to do it, but I have to do something to make you forget the guy." Angrily he looked at the folder. "I walked into your room to see what kind of letters he was writing to you to make you look so happy about getting them and I found this folder. At first I thought these were copies of letters you wrote to him, but when I read what he wrote to you, I knew better. I knew these were letters that you wanted to send to him but didn't dare."

"I hate you, Ben," she said in a low, tense voice.

"Just so you forget about Scott!"

"And do you think this will make me forget? I love him, Ben. I will always love him." The words echoed in her mind as she realized they were the very words that Susan had used about Joe and now Jerry.

"He'll never look at you again once he reads these."

She lunged toward him and caught him off guard and knocked him down. He struck his head sharply against the desk and cried out in pain. Blood spurted from a strange gash right at his hairline and she stared at it in panic.

"My head," he said weakly as he pushed himself up. "It's bleeding." He looked at the blood on his hand as if he'd never seen blood before. "I'm bleeding." As if in slow motion, he reached into the gym bag standing open on the floor. He pulled out a small towel and pressed it against the gash.

"Oh, dear! What shall I do?" She looked at his head, then at the folder beside the fallen chair. The towel was becoming stained with red.

"Get Dad, but do it quietly so nobody else comes up here."

She snatched up her folder, then glared down at him. "I hope you bleed all over the carpet! I hope you have to have fifty stitches!"

"Are you going to call Dad?"

"I'll think about it." She dashed from the room, her heart racing alarmingly. She couldn't just leave Ben like that. She pushed the folder out of sight under her bed, then ran downstairs.

Finally she found Chuck in the study talking to Steve. Chuck looked up and smiled, then the smile faded. "What is it, Elizabeth?"

"I need you for a minute." Her voice shook, but she couldn't help it.

"Excuse me, Steve. Why don't you find the ladies until I get finished with this family matter?" Chuck rattled the change in his pocket as he smiled at Steve.

Elizabeth could barely stand still. As soon as Steve was out of hearing, she caught Chuck's hand and told him to hurry upstairs to Ben.

"What happened to upset you this much?" he asked as they rushed up.

"I—I accidently pushed Ben and he hit his head."

Chuck muttered something under his breath and Elizabeth wanted to run to her room and hide, but she walked into Ben's room and watched as Chuck examined Ben.

"I think it looks worse than it is. We'll wash it off and see about it." He helped Ben to the bathroom down the hall and Elizabeth couldn't leave until she knew how bad it was.

After Chuck washed it off, he stuck a butterfly bandage over it and then quietly asked the Lord to heal it. Then he studied Ben. "What did you do that made Elizabeth push you so hard?"

"Nothing!" cried Elizabeth in alarm.

"I asked Ben," said Chuck sharply.

"I—I had something of hers that she wanted back," said Ben with his head down.

Chuck was quiet a long time and then finally said, "You two will have to settle this yourselves. You're old enough now to handle these things on your own. Talk it out, apologize, forgive each other, then forget it." He kissed Ben, then Elizabeth. "I'll see you downstairs later."

Elizabeth watched Chuck walk away; then she looked at Ben, her eyes narrowed. "I have nothing to say to you."

"I can still tell Scott about the letters even if I don't have them to show to him."

Elizabeth glared at Ben, her hands on her

hips. "Would you really do that, Ben? I sure didn't think you would ever do anything to hurt me."

"Hurt you! I am helping you!"

"You are not! You're making things worse. Why can't you understand? Why do you have to treat me this way? I won't give up my piano because I love Scott!" She had to convince Ben to keep quiet about the letters!

Slowly Ben walked down the hall to his room again. Elizabeth followed, her mind racing. Ben turned at his door. "You're not welcome in my room. Go back to your room and dream about Scott."

"Please, Ben." She reached out to him, but he backed away. "Ben! You have to promise me that you won't talk to Scott about me or my letters."

Ben shook his head. "I'll promise if you forget him."

"How can I turn off my feelings and my thoughts?"

"Just do it. Think about winning that piano competition next month. That's what's important for you."

"I know what's important!" She wanted to scream and never stop, or throw herself down and kick her heels the way she used to do.

Ben sighed. "If you practice enough, then I won't tell him."

She stiffened. "What do you call enough?"

He shrugged. "I'll know by listening to you."

"No! You'll make me too nervous now. How will I know if I'm doing a good job? How will I know that you won't tell him no matter what?"

"I said I wouldn't, didn't I?"

She leaned toward him, her eyes slits of anger. "I don't trust you, Ben Johnson! I'll never trust you again!"

She spun around, walked to her room, and slammed the door behind her.

Eleven
Practice

Elizabeth missed a note, then crashed her hands down on the keys in frustration. How could she practice with Ben's threat always in her mind? Maybe she should find Ben and tell him that she was dropping piano altogether, and just see how much he liked that!

A log snapped in the fireplace and she jumped. Someone laughed from another room. She frowned. Would *she* ever laugh again?

Slowly she flexed her long fingers, then once again tried to play. She fumbled, then started again. She felt as she had when she'd first started piano lessons. The music was in her head, but she couldn't make it come out her fingers. How could she enter the competition? The judges and audience would laugh at her, then she'd walk off the stage in disgrace. Joanne Tripper would never let her forget it.

"Oh! Oh, dear!" Elizabeth covered her face with her hands, then jumped as a hand squeezed her shoulder.

"Would you tell a friend what's wrong?" asked Scott softly.

She wanted to throw her arms around him and sob against his broad chest, but she only shook her head.

"We're friends, Elizabeth. I want to know what's troubling you. I want to know why you're so tense that you can't play this song, the same song that I heard you playing yesterday without a mistake," He sat on the bench beside her and she wanted to run from the room to get away from him.

"I guess I can concentrate better on some days. I really should go start chores now." She moved but he caught her and held her in place.

"Are you angry with me, Elizabeth?"

She gasped. Finally she said, "Should I be?"

He shook his dark head. "I want us to be friends. I don't want anything to break up our friendship."

"Not even Rhonda?" Elizabeth asked coldly, looking Scott right in the eyes.

He flushed slightly. "I have a special feeling for Rhonda, but that shouldn't stop us from being friends."

Elizabeth looked down at her hands. Her back ached from being so tense. Maybe this would be the best time to stop her association with Scott. She moistened her dry lips with the tip of her tongue. "Scott, I'm going to be very busy with my career. I—I don't think I'll have time to write to you anymore."

"Not even once in a while?"

She wanted to burst into tears. He wanted her to write! "I don't know how I'll have the time. I want to give all my time and energy to piano." The words almost stuck in her throat and she didn't dare look at Scott's expression. She felt him stiffen and it was like a blow to her heart.

"I'll miss your letters," he said in a low voice. "You encourage me a lot. I'll drop you a note once in a while, and if you do find the time, you write back."

Oh, that Ben! He'd pay for this!

Suddenly Ben walked into the room, his face red with anger. Elizabeth jumped up and caught at his arm to drag him away, but he jerked out of her reach.

"I told you, Elizabeth, and you wouldn't listen. It's too late now."

"No, Ben!"

Scott stood beside the piano and looked from one to the other. "What's

94

the problem? I've never seen you two fighting before."

"We'll settle it, Scott," said Elizabeth, shaking uncontrollably. "Ben just misunderstood what I was doing."

"I did not! I warned you, didn't I? I said I'd do something for your own good."

Her eyes flashed and she stood with her feet apart, her fists doubled tightly. "I'll never forgive you, Ben!"

"I think you two had better calm down and sit down and discuss this quietly," said Scott as he reached for Ben's arm.

Ben glared at Scott. "It's your fault, too!"

"What is?"

Elizabeth groaned and wanted to run from the room, but she couldn't leave Ben in the same room with Scott. "Ben, I can explain if you'd give me a chance!"

He shook his head with a scowl. "It's too late." He looked at Scott and Elizabeth grabbed for Ben, but he jumped out of her reach. "Scott, do you know how Elizabeth is wasting the time she needs for practicing piano?"

"No." Scott scratched his head. "What's gotten into you, Ben? You are upsetting Elizabeth."

"Don't say another word, Ben!" cried Elizabeth almost in hysterics. How could she get him to keep quiet? Silently she asked the Lord to help her, and to change Ben's mind. Right now she needed a miracle, and she knew the Lord had answered her prayers many times in the past.

Ben turned to Elizabeth, his face flushed with anger. At the sight of her tearstained face, his expression changed. He made a choking sound, then turned and walked out of the room.

Elizabeth stared open-mouthed after him, then snapped her mouth shut as tears of thanksgiving to God filled her eyes. Once again God had answered her! Silently she thanked him, then dabbed away her tears.

"What was that all about?" asked Scott, shaking his head.

She smiled at him. "It's over now. I'm sorry that we were fighting. I'm sure Ben's sorry, too."

Just then Rhonda walked in. "Oh, Scott! There you are. I've been looking for you." She squeezed his hand and smiled into his eyes, then looked at Elizabeth with a smile. "Will you play for us now?"

Elizabeth agreed, then almost fell over in surprise. She'd actually agreed to play for Rhonda and Scott together! What was happening to her? She was probably so happy that God had answered her prayer that she'd agree to anything.

She watched Scott and Rhonda sit side by side on the couch, holding hands, and no pain shot through her. She just sat at the piano and played without a mistake. Later she'd have to think about all of this, but for now it felt heavenly to play without the pressure that she'd been feeling.

Later after she'd finished her chores, she walked to the cow barn to find Ben. He stood near the faucet rinsing out the milker, "Ben."

He looked over his shoulder, then quickly away, his face red.

She stood beside him until he tipped the milker up to drain. "Ben, thank you for not telling Scott."

He pulled off his cap and rubbed his head, then tugged his cap in place. "I—I was wrong, Elizabeth."

Her heart seemed to stop. "About not telling him?"

Ben shook his head. "About taking the folder of letters. About everything. I shouldn't have gone to your room to look at your private letters. I shouldn't have been upset about your practice time. I know you practice a lot. I just didn't want anything to keep you from doing what you wanted to do."

"Nothing will, Ben," she whispered, blinking back tears. A cow mooed and a barn cat meowed near Ben's foot. "I will practice my piano more and more. I want to be the best pianist ever."

He nodded. "I know how important it is to you, and it's important to me. I want others to know that Elizabeth Johnson is special! I want them to forget that you were ever Libby Dobbs, aid kid."

She touched his arm. "Ben, it doesn't matter if they remember that I was an aid kid. Maybe it's better if they do; then everyone will know that even a dirty, little aid kid can really make her dream come true. And if I can make my dream come true, other kids can, too, even aid kids who think there is no hope."

"You're right, Elizabeth. I never thought about that." He leaned against a support post. "Some of the boys in school tease me about having you for a sister. They say once an aid kid always an aid kid. I told them that you're my sister now and that you're going to be famous someday. They laugh and make fun of me. They'll sure find out when you win that piano competition next month!"

"But Ben, what if I don't win?"

His jaw tightened. "You'll win!"

"But there are twenty-four others playing!"

"You'll win!"

She tugged off her gloves and stuffed them into her pocket. "Ben, even if I lose, I'll still be a concert pianist someday. I will!"

He twisted his boot. "Two guys are taking bets that you'll lose."

Her eyes widened. "That's terrible! You didn't bet, did you?"

He shook his head. "I told them if I did bet that I'd bet that you'd win. They just laughed. Oh, Elizabeth, I want you to win!"

"I want to win." She turned away, her shoulders drooping. What would happen to Ben if she lost?

"I know you'll win," Ben called after her.

She stopped in the yard and breathed deeply of the cold night air. The yard light brightened a large circle of yard. A car drove past; then all was quiet.

What would she do if she lost the competition?

Twelve
A letter from Scott

Elizabeth flexed her fingers, then turned away from the baby grand piano after her hour of independent study. Scott would be very proud of her if he'd heard today's practice.

She smiled dreamily as she remembered his tight hug when he'd left their house last month after Thanksgiving weekend. He'd whispered, "I hope to hear from you soon." She'd nodded, then peeked at Ben. He hadn't smiled, but he hadn't frowned either.

"I'll do my best to come to your competition," Scott had said as he slid into his car to drive away.

She sighed and hugged her books to her chest as she walked away from the piano. With Scott in the audience, she'd play even better. Maybe she would win.

Just then the door opened and Jerry Grosbeck walked in. He was dressed in jeans and a medium blue sweater shirt. "Hi," he said, smiling.

Her heart gave an awkward fumbling leap and she managed a smile. "Hi." Why did she feel so strange around Jerry?

"I stood outside and listened to you."

"You did?" Suddenly she frowned. "What are you doing in here? You can't come in here and bother me!"

He laughed. "Do I bother you? I never would have guessed."

She didn't know what to do with him in this mood. "You'd better get to your class."

"I have a pass to leave study hall. I wanted to hear you again. And I wanted to talk to you. Susan's been hanging around me so much that I never get to talk to you."

"I noticed."

"You did?" His eyes lit up.

She ducked her head, suddenly feeling awkward and shy. "Susan doesn't care who knows that she likes you."

He laughed as he tugged Elizabeth's curl. "Susan and I had a long talk this morning. We have an understanding."

Elizabeth's shoulders tensed. Did that mean Jerry and Susan were going together? But who could hold out against

101

Susan for very long? Any boy would be glad to go with her.

"Don't you want to hear about our understanding?" asked Jerry with a grin.

Elizabeth lifted her pointed chin. "I am not interested, Jerry Grosbeck! I am only interested in my piano."

"And in Scott Norris," Jerry said gruffly.

She looked at Jerry in surprise. Why should he care as long as she didn't let Scott get in the way of her piano?

Just then the bell rang and Elizabeth hurried to the door.

"I'll see you tomorrow, Libby."

She looked back at him, her hand on the doorknob. "Tomorrow's the first day of Christmas vacation. There's no school."

He smiled. "I know. I'm riding out to your place tomorrow to visit."

"Oh." Why did she feel excited? Was it because of Jerry's visit or because of the start of Christmas vacation, which would give her more time to practice for the competition?

"If it's not too cold, can we go horseback riding?"

"You and Susan?"

He tapped the tip of her nose. "You and me."

She jerked open the door and rushed

out, her heart racing. Why was Jerry doing this to her? Since he loved Susan so much, why didn't he go riding with her?

"See you tomorrow," he called after her and she quickened her pace. Why did he make her feel so strange? Why hadn't he just stayed that little runny-nosed aid kid with the torn clothes?

She stopped in the restroom and splashed cold water on her flushed face, then blotted it dry. She looked in the mirror, then caught the reflection of Joanne Tripper and she wanted to run.

"Momma says you won't be playing in the competition," said Joanne, tugging the belt on her slacks more tightly. "She is going to have a serious talk with Rachael Avery and with the two judges she knows. You'll be out of that competition for sure."

Elizabeth shook her head, forcing herself to keep her temper. "You can't do anything and your momma can't either. I am going to play, and nothing will stop me!"

"Momma's going to make sure the judges know all about your life before you lived with the Johnsons. And she'll tell them all about your real mother, Marie Dobbs. They will want to know what kind of mother you have."

Elizabeth clenched her fists. She would not knock Joanne down! "My mother is Vera Johnson, and you know it!"

"You might as well withdraw your name, Libby, and save yourself a lot of embarrassment."

She walked out the door before she lost control and pushed Joanne into the toilet.

Mrs. Tripper couldn't really do anything, could she?

Elizabeth stopped at her locker and pushed her books inside, then stood there with her head down. "Please, heavenly Father, take care of me," she whispered hoarsely. "Don't let Joanne or her mother cause trouble for me."

Elizabeth remembered the other times the Lord had answered her, and she relaxed and smiled and told him thank you for love and help and strength.

For the rest of the day and the next whenever she thought about Joanne and her threats, she thanked the Lord for taking care of it. Then she stopped worrying.

She looked down at Rex by her side as she walked to the mailbox and said, "Everything is going to be just fine, Rex. In a few days we'll have Christmas and then the competition. I'm ready for it. I know I'm playing really well."

Rex barked a short, sharp bark as if he were agreeing and she laughed happily. Today seemed like such a perfect day for some reason.

She pulled out the mail and looked through it, then laughed aloud. She had a letter from Scott! He hadn't written since Thanksgiving, and she suddenly realized that she'd completely forgotten to write to him.

As she walked up the long drive she opened the letter and read:

Dear Elizabeth,

It won't be long now before the competition. I know you have a strong chance to win. I'm really sorry, but I can't make it after all. Rhonda and I made special plans. But be sure to tell me all about it, won't you?

Rhonda agreed to marry me. We're going to wait until she's out of school this spring. I know she's the wife God has for me, and she knows I'm the husband God has for her. It happened so suddenly that it is hard to comprehend yet. That will make us cousins, won't it, Elizabeth?

I'm working on a new song that I'm very happy with. I just started taking voice lessons. One of these days I'll be singing my own songs for records as well as doing concerts. Rhonda will enjoy that since she likes my music.

I had a short talk with your friend Jerry before I left your place last month. He's a nice boy, Elizabeth. He likes you a lot.

I'll be praying for you on the day of the

competition. Let me know how it comes out.

Have a very merry Christmas. I'm spending Christmas with Rhonda. Good-bye for now.

> *Your friend,*
> *Scott*

She held the letter, looking down at it, and waited for the pain to sweep over her. Nothing happened. In fact, she was glad for Scott and Rhonda. Now, wasn't that funny? Why wasn't she upset? Why wasn't she in tears right now?

"Elizabeth Gail Johnson!"

She turned and her heart leaped as Jerry rode up beside her. "Hi, Jerry. Susan's in the house waiting for you."

"She is?" He walked his bike along beside her. He nodded toward the letter in her hand. "Is that a letter from the great Scott Norris?"

She colored. "Yes."

He grabbed it, and she didn't try to grab it back. "I'm going to read this great love letter."

"Who cares?"

He looked at her with a funny look on his face, then quickly read the letter. "So, he's going to marry Rhonda. I'm glad of that."

"I'm sorry he can't come to the competition."

"Me, too," he said dryly. He stood the bike near the garage. "I guess I'd better see what Susan wants."

"I guess you'd better." Elizabeth walked inside and hung up her jacket. Reluctantly she walked away from Jerry and found Vera in the study. "Here's the mail, Mom. I got a letter from Scott if you want to read that."

"I'd like to if you don't mind." Vera picked up the pack of mail and quickly looked through it, then took the letter from Scott.

Smells of the Christmas tree filled the room and blended with Vera's perfume. It didn't seem much like Christmas because the competition was always in Elizabeth's mind. At least she had her Christmas shopping done.

Vera handed back the letter. "I'm not surprised that he and Rhonda are planning on getting married. They'll make a fine couple."

Elizabeth nodded. Why wasn't she sobbing? Why wasn't her heart broken? Didn't she love Scott?

"Scott will fit right into our family, won't he? Now there'll be two of us with musical ability." Vera studied Elizabeth thoughtfully. "Do you want to talk to me, honey? You look as if something is on your mind."

Elizabeth gnawed her bottom lip. "I love Scott, Mom."

"I know, honey. We all do. I just wonder if you know that there are different kinds of love. Rhonda loves Scott the way a woman loves a man. You love Scott as a special friend who shares your love of music and that creates a special bond. I love Scott as a dear member of our family even though he doesn't belong yet."

"Am I too young to be in love, Mom?" Elizabeth fingered a pencil on Chuck's desk.

"I don't think so." Vera walked around the desk and slipped her arm around Elizabeth. "Maybe you won't have the kind of mature love it takes for marriage, but you could be in love with someone. Are you, hon?"

Elizabeth sighed and shook her head. "I guess not. I thought I was in love with Scott, but I was wrong."

"You have plenty of time to fall in love."

"Susan's always falling in love."

Vera chuckled and nodded. "I know, but you're different from Susan. You are more serious-minded than she is."

"I guess I wouldn't want to be Susan any more than she'd want to be me. I might go riding with Jerry if he remembers that he asked me."

"Is Jerry here?"

"Yes. He's talking to Susan now. Maybe she'll want to go riding with us."

Vera frowned thoughtfully as she tugged her sweater over her jeans. "I thought Susan was having someone over this afternoon to play Ping-Pong."

Probably Jerry. Elizabeth walked out of the study listlessly. She might as well go to her room since Susan was going to take all of Jerry's time.

Slowly she walked upstairs to her bedroom. She dropped the letter from Scott on her desk instead of neatly filing it away with the others. She walked to the window and stood looking out with her forehead pressed against the cold glass.

Thirteen
Elizabeth's heart

With a heavy sigh Elizabeth walked to her desk and sat down. Maybe she should write a letter to Scott. She pulled out the yellow folder and opened it, then slowly read each letter that she'd written.

Had she really written all that love stuff? What a child she had been!

She picked up the top letter and tore it into small pieces and dropped it into her red wastebasket. She picked up the next letter and did the same. Finally every love letter to Scott was torn into pieces.

She shook her head and sighed again. For a whole year she'd thought she was in love with Scott. Well, she did love him. She just hadn't been *in* love with him. Or maybe she had been just a little, but the love couldn't grow so it had changed directions.

She stuffed today's letter from Scott into the drawer where she kept all the letters she'd received, then closed the drawer. She'd write to Scott after the competition.

She walked listlessly around her bedroom, automatically tugging a wrinkle out of her well-made bed and moving her hairbrush to its place. What would she do with the day if Jerry was spending his time with Susan? Why had he said he was coming to ride with her, if he had really come to play Ping-Pong with Susan?

Elizabeth stopped at her window and watched Rex walk across the yard. She should have gone with Ben and the boys in the wagon to help a customer choose a Christmas tree. She had watched Ben hitch up Jack and Dan and wished that she could go, but she wouldn't have time to ride up with Ben and ride with Jerry. So she'd waited for Jerry. And why had she? He had forgotten that he'd said they'd go riding today. Susan had made him forget everything!

"I'll just go riding alone!"

She might as well, since she was dressed for it. Jerry could stay with Susan and play Ping-Pong until he turned into a small white ball for all she cared.

She walked downstairs, then hesitated at the closed basement door. Slowly, quietly she opened the door and listened. She could hear muffled talking and the ball striking the table. Susan and Jerry were down there! Just as slowly and quietly Elizabeth closed the door, then stood there, with her head down. With a sigh she turned and headed for the barn.

She felt numb as she pulled on her jacket, then her riding boots. She'd be all right as soon as she was on Snowball's back riding through the field. Why should she care that Jerry chose to stay with Susan? Wouldn't any boy?

As Elizabeth stepped outdoors, the cold air rushed against her and turned her pale cheeks pink. Goosy Poosy looked at her, then chose to ignore her. Rex pushed his nose against her leg and thumped his tail.

"Would you like to go with me, Rex? We'll entertain each other. We don't need anyone, do we?" She looked wistfully back at the house. It would have been nice to ride with Jerry. Oh, well. She had Rex, and she'd be riding Snowball. They were company enough.

Forcing a spring to her step, she walked to the horse barn where she'd left Snowball and Apache Girl so they'd be easy to saddle. Now, she'd turn Apache Girl into the pen with Star and the ponies.

She pushed open the barn door and stepped in, leaving Rex outside. The barn was dark and the pungent odor made Elizabeth wrinkle her nose as she clicked on the light.

112

"I wondered how long it would take you to get out here."

Her eyes widened and her heart leaped. "Jerry!"

"Why are you so surprised? We have a riding date—remember?" He smiled at her as he stood near Snowball's stall. He was dressed in jeans and a heavy corduroy jacket that matched his dark hair and eyes.

She walked toward him on unsteady legs. "But I heard you in the basement with Susan. You were playing Ping-Pong."

Jerry laughed and shook his head. "Susan and Dave Boomer are in the basement playing Ping-Pong."

"But what about you? She loves you."

"I told you we have an understanding."

Elizabeth tugged off her gloves and stuffed them roughly in her jacket pocket. "I get it. She'll let you go riding with me today, but she wants you back tomorrow."

Jerry laughed. "Are you jealous?"

She glared at him, her fists on her hips. "What a dumb thing to say! I am not jealous!" But she suddenly realized she was. But why? She turned quickly away and fumbled for the bridle. This was ridiculous. She had no reason to be jealous.

Jerry slipped a bridle on Apache Girl as Elizabeth slipped one on Snowball. Snowball nickered and tried to nuzzle Elizabeth.

She grabbed the saddle and hoisted it in place, then tightened the cinch. "Do you need help, Jerry?" she asked coldly.

"Ben showed me how, Libby. Have you forgotten that Ben and I have ridden a lot together?"

She sniffed, then tugged the reins for Snowball to follow her out of the barn. She blinked against the sunlight. The sky was bright blue and she knew another day would go by without snow.

Elizabeth swung into the saddle, then watched Jerry mount easily. She remembered the first time she'd sat on the back of a horse. The ground had seemed a mile away. Now, riding was as easy as walking.

After they'd ridden for a while, Jerry said, "If someone had told us five years ago that we'd be on a farm riding horses we'd have called them all kinds of dirty names."

Elizabeth chuckled as she looked over at Jerry. "We'd have gotten mad because we had no hope then. We thought we would be ragged aid kids forever, with no one to love us. And now look. I'm glad for our lives now! I'm glad we have enough to eat and warm clothes to wear and someone to love us."

Jerry nodded, his face serious. "Maybe someday we can help kids like us."

She smiled at him as she suddenly

realized just how kind he was. "I would like that, Jerry." He smiled at her and she felt breathless as she nudged Snowball into a trot.

They met Ben and the boys driving back in the wagon, a large Christmas tree sticking out the back. Jack and Dan nickered to Snowball and Apache Girl and they answered.

"Have fun," called Ben, lifting his hand. His face was red with cold.

Kevin and Toby sat beside Ben and the Tanner family sat on the second seat, looking very pleased and excited.

The noise of the wagon faded in the distance, and Jerry said. "Let's ride to the Christmas trees, shall we? We'll pretend we're here to choose a tree. Remember when we were kids how we loved looking at the trees decorated in town?"

She nodded. "But the trees in our homes never looked pretty, did they? Maybe it was because we were never allowed to help decorate them."

"I'm glad that's behind us. Now, we're happy—both of us. And we are loved." Once again he smiled his warm, gentle smile and Elizabeth had to look away. Did he know what he was doing to her?

At Ben's Christmas trees Elizabeth dismounted, then tied the reins to a tree branch. She turned as Jerry did the same.

He held his hand out to her. She hesitated, her stomach fluttering strangely; then she gave him her hand. His hand closed around hers as if they'd always walked hand in hand.

"This is a beautiful tree," said Jerry, pointing to a blue spruce just a little taller than he.

"All of them are beautiful." Elizabeth looked around at the rows and rows of Christmas trees, then at the seedlings that Kevin and Toby had planted last spring.

"Ben has quite a business. He said by the time he's ready for college, he'll have enough money saved from all the years of selling Christmas trees to pay all his expenses."

"He's really worked hard, but he likes doing it."

"Look at the cardinal, Elizabeth," whispered Jerry, pointing at the bright red bird on a green branch.

"It's beautiful."

Slowly they walked among the trees and Elizabeth was glad that Dave Boomer, instead of Jerry, was playing Ping-Pong with Susan. She smiled at Jerry and he squeezed her hand.

"I think it's time we talked," he said facing her and taking her other hand.

She stiffened. "About what?"

"Mine and Susan's arrangement."

116

"Oh." Elizabeth didn't know if she wanted to hear it.

"I told Susan that she and I could be friends, but that she'd have to find someone else to go with because I love another girl."

"You turned Susan down?"

"Don't be surprised. Not every boy prefers short, redheaded girls. Some of us like tall, brown-haired girls with hazel eyes."

Her heart hammered against her rib cage. Could he mean her?

"I love you, Elizabeth Gail Johnson."

"Me?" She knew her eyes were very round and that her mouth was open in an o. Was he teasing her the way he had in the past? If she believed him, would he start laughing and tell her that she'd fall for any trick?

He cupped her face with his hand. His eyes looked soft and full of love and she didn't want to move away from him even if he were teasing her. "I think you are the most courageous girl I know. You work hard at your dream. You are sweet and good and kind."

"Me?"

He laughed gently. "Don't look so surprised. I know the real Libby Johnson. I knew you when you were Libby Dobbs." He lowered his head and gently kissed her.

Her heart seemed to stop, then raced on. He did love her, and not Susan!

"Can't you tell me how you feel, Libby? It really is all right." He ran his finger down the side of her face and she shivered at his touch.

Suddenly she knew how she felt about him. She knew what she'd kept hidden even to herself. "I love you, Jerry."

He pulled her close and she slipped her arms around his neck. His warm lips touched hers and she returned his kiss with her whole heart.

Fourteen
Competition

Rachel Avery clasped Elizabeth's hands firmly. "I'm glad you're finally here! I was beginning to worry."

"We had to wait for Toby to get ready. The whole family wanted to be here."

Rachel stood back from Elizabeth and looked her up and down. "You look fantastic in that long green dress. Very festive. And your hair is beautiful."

"I just wish I wasn't so nervous." Elizabeth rubbed her arms and tried to quiet the rapid beat of her heart. She looked around at the other students waiting to play. She was scheduled to be the seventeenth competitor. She crumpled her music nervously, then rubbed it straight. One more hour and she would play in front of the judges and the audience. Joanne Tripper was the twentieth player.

Elizabeth peeked around to see if Joanne was nearby, but she couldn't see the blonde girl among the people backstage.

"Relax, Elizabeth." Rachael patted Elizabeth's shoulder. Rachael looked very pretty with her dark hair piled on top of her head. Her long wine-colored dress almost touched the floor. "There is a lot of tension in the air, but you must keep your mind free of it. You are going to walk out there and play your piece and enjoy it. You're going to play your very best."

She nodded, then listened to the person playing now. Elizabeth shuddered. Could she hope to play better than the boy playing now? He was very good. Were the judges tired of listening after all this time?

"Let's sit down, Elizabeth. You'll be worn out if we stand here or pace back and forth." Rachael led the way to chairs arranged for the competitors.

Elizabeth sat down, then jumped up. "I want to find the bathroom and check myself over one more time."

"I'll hold your music. Please come right back. I feel better with you right here beside me. If you don't go onstage when your name is called, then you automatically forfeit an opportunity to play."

"I'll be back. Don't worry."

Carefully Elizabeth picked her way around the things backstage and walked to the end of a narrow hall to the restroom.

Suddenly someone grabbed her and pushed her into a small, dimly lighted room. She called out and grabbed for the door, but it was shut and a key grated in the lock. She gasped in panic, her heart racing, her skin crawling with fear.

"I said you wouldn't get to play!" It was Joanne Tripper!

"Let me out, Joanne! I mean it!"

"I'll let you out when it's too late for you to play." Joanne laughed. Then all was quiet.

Elizabeth rattled the knob, but the door wouldn't open. She fumbled around and found a light and turned it on. The room was a small dressing room that looked as if it hadn't been cleaned for a long time. There were no windows and no other door.

"How can I get out?"

Tears stung her eyes as she slowly walked around, almost tripping over a wooden chair with a broken leg. Oh, that Joanne Tripper had gone too far this time!

Elizabeth doubled her fists at her sides, and stamped her foot. Her skin pricked with perspiration.

"Calm down and think, Elizabeth," she muttered. If Ben or Kevin were here they'd think of a way out.

Just then she heard voices outside the

door. She rushed to the door and banged against it, but nothing happened. Didn't they hear her? Or didn't they care? Was everyone so concerned about the piano competition that they couldn't hear a girl in distress?

"Rachael will come for me. She knows I said I'd be right back. Sure, she'll come." But maybe she wouldn't come right away. Elizabeth frowned and gnawed at her bottom lip. She had to get out so that she could relax before she had to go onstage and play.

Tears filled her eyes, but she forced them back. She would not ruin her makeup! She would get out of here and get back to Rachael and wait her turn to play.

She breathed deeply, then sneezed from the dust in the room. How could this happen to her?

If Jerry knew that she was in trouble, he'd be here on the double. He would take care of Joanne Tripper!

Elizabeth locked her fingers together and paced back and forth near the door. Suddenly she lifted her head as she remembered that she wasn't alone even in this difficulty. God was with her always! He'd answered her prayers many times before, and he'd answer again.

"Heavenly Father, please help me get out of here," she whispered. "I know that I must forgive Joanne even if I don't want to. Please send someone to unlock this door so I can get out. I pray in Jesus' name. Thank you, Father."

She watched the door for a while, then turned and walked across the small room. She turned again to watch the door, then walked back to it. She leaned her forehead against the door frame and waited. As she stood there she heard footsteps. Her heart almost jumped out of her dress. Frantic, she pounded on the door and yelled, "Please open the door. I'm locked in! Let me out!"

She heard a key grate in the lock and she trembled violently. Someone was unlocking the door! She stepped aside and the door swung in.

"Libby!"

"Jerry!" She flung her arms around him and pressed her face against his neck. "Oh, Jerry!"

His arms tightened around her. "How did you get in there?"

She lifted her face. "How did you find me?"

"I talked to Rachael Avery because I wanted to wish you well before your turn to play. You weren't there and she was getting worried about you, so I came to find you."

"I've got to go to the restroom and make

sure I look all right, but wait for me." She started to walk away, but he caught her hand.

"Who locked you in?"

She licked her lips. "Joanne."

"She is not fit to be here! I'm going to talk to her right now and stop her from performing."

"No, Jerry. There is so much tension in the air now. If you make a big deal out of this, no one will be able to perform well. We'll leave it until later, then settle it."

He frowned, then reluctantly agreed.

Later she walked back to Rachael with Jerry. Rachael rushed to her and grabbed her hands.

"I was frantic! You have about five minutes before you go on. Oh, my dear, don't ever disappear like that again."

"I won't." She turned and caught Joanne's eyes. Joanne crept behind her mother and Elizabeth sank down on her chair to catch her breath.

"I'll be in the audience with your parents," whispered Jerry. He winked at her then hurried away.

Silently she asked the Lord to help her play her piece to the best of her ability, then thanked him for taking such good care of her.

She heard her name announced and she stood up with her head high and her

124

shoulders square. Rachael pushed the music into her hands and she walked onstage to the baby grand piano.

She positioned her music, then turned and bowed and smiled at the audience as they applauded. She sat on the bench and rested her hands on the keys. A hush settled over the audience; then she began to play. The music rose from the piano and spread through her body. She knew she was playing better than she'd ever played before.

Several minutes later she stood and once again bowed and smiled. The audience clapped until she was backstage. Rachael grabbed her and hugged her and kissed both her cheeks. Elizabeth hugged Rachael and kissed her, then burst into tears.

At seven o'clock Elizabeth sat with the other competitors on the chairs onstage opposite the piano as Mr. Hedges gave his short speech about how the competition had started six years ago and how proud he was to be a part of it.

Elizabeth locked her fingers together in her lap and could barely sit still as she listened.

"The judges have reached a decision," said Mr. Hedges brightly. "They said it was hard to choose because all of you were very good." He smiled at the competitors and Elizabeth couldn't force herself to smile in return. Her face felt frozen in place. She wanted to peek out in the audience to try to find her family and Jerry, but she didn't dare move.

Finally Mr. Hedges announced the fourth, third, and second place winners. Elizabeth didn't know the two boys and the girl. They thanked the judges and Mr. Hedges and then sat down again.

"The winner is a very fortunate young lady. This will help her career a great deal." Mr. Hedges chuckled as if to say that he knew he was prolonging someone's agony.

"The winner is Elizabeth Johnson!"

She gasped, then stood up and managed to walk to Mr. Hedges without falling flat on her face in front of everyone. She shook his hand and said thank you, then looked out and smiled at the applauding audience. She had won! Elizabeth Gail Johnson was truly on her way to becoming a famous concert pianist.

She walked to the piano to play "Theme from the Surprise Symphony" by Haydn as Rachael had instructed her to do if she won. She bowed and smiled at the audience. She saw Jerry and he kissed his fingertips and turned his hand toward her and she knew that he'd sent her a kiss. She smiled right at him, then sat down and once again played for the audience, for her family, and for Jerry.

126